Clarity

Loretta Lost

ISBN-13: 978-1497525344
ISBN-10: 1497525349
Copyright © 2014 Loretta Lost.
Cover image by Sarah Hansen.
All rights reserved.

Will our life not be a tunnel between two vague clarities? Or will it not be a clarity between two dark triangles?

- Pablo Neruda

Table of Contents

Chapter 1 .... *1*

Chapter 2 .... *18*

Chapter 3 .... *29*

Chapter 4 .... *53*

Chapter 5 .... *85*

Chapter 6 .... *99*

Chapter 7 .... *108*

Chapter 8 .... *117*

Chapter 9 .... *123*

Chapter 10 .... *133*

Chapter 11 .... *142*

CLARITY 2

Chapter One

Everything is soft, dark, and peaceful. I sway in suspension, comforted by the silence. A sweet, feminine voice calls for me from somewhere distant. Only then do I become aware that I have been sitting on the ground and staring forward vacantly for several minutes. I have withdrawn so deep inside myself that even several sharp knocks on the bathroom door cannot draw me out of my stupor.

"Hellie?" a woman says with a sniffle. "Are you okay? I heard a crash."

I try to respond, but I am locked inside the maze of my own mind. I try to navigate toward the sound and climb out of my subconscious, but there are thick stone walls all around me. I keep slipping back down into my quiet, isolated pit of protection. The voices on the outside sound faraway and muffled, and I can't reach them. I don't know if I want to reach them; it's safe here. Still, there is something tugging at the edge of my soul and reminding me that I have an urgent responsibility.

Loretta Lost

I try to remember what it is, but my brain feels like slush. I can't speak. I can't think.

"Who's in there?" Grayson asks. "One of your bridesmaids?"

"No," Carmen says. "It's my sister."

He pauses. "Your sister's here? Your blind sister Helen?"

Carmen huffs in exasperation. "Yes, Gray. Who else would I be talking about? I don't have any other sisters."

"I—I just..." Grayson makes a sharp and jagged intake of air. He seems suddenly agitated and alarmed. "You—you said she wasn't coming. You said you hadn't seen her in years. You said she wouldn't..." He gulps so loudly that I can hear the saliva barreling down the tunnel of his throat. I imagine the liquid swirling and sizzling into steam as it mixes with the raging hellfire of guilt in his gut. "You said she wouldn't be at our wedding."

"Yes, but she called me last night," Carmen says softly. "I told her to come home and be my maid of honor. Helen!" she calls again, rapping gently on the bathroom door. "Sweetie, is everything okay?"

A searing pain pierces behind my eyes and abruptly brings me back to reality. I blink rapidly. I lift my fingers shakily to touch the side of my head. There is a bit of warm, sticky moisture seeping between the strands of my hair, and a quickly forming bump just over my temple. I

CLARITY 2

wince, and rest my elbow on the side of the bathtub so I can keep my hand pressed against my forehead. *Okay, Helen. There's no time for you to fall apart. Get it together. You need to think clearly. Quickly.* Try as I might, I can't seem to make heads or tails of the situation. My heart is racing, my breathing is labored and uneven, and my whole body is shaking with silent fury.

"I thought you hated your sister," Grayson whispers. "I thought—I thought you were angry that she left without a word. She doesn't give a shit about you! Why would you invite her here?"

"I was just pretending to be pissed to hide how hurt I was. She's my best friend! I missed her nonstop, every day." Carmen is close to the point of tears again, and I hear her voice breaking. "What the fuck is wrong with you, Gray? Don't you know me?"

"I'm sorry, honey. Come here."

My ears are assaulted with the sound of them embracing again. I can hear him pressing kisses against her face to soothe her, and each time their skin connects, I feel my insides churning in disgust. The cupcakes in my stomach rebel at being confined within their gastric prison, and fight to make their exit in a gushing eruption. I clamp my hands around my middle and shut my eyes tightly, trying to avoid duplicating Carmen's performance from the morning—it will not help this situation in the least if I need to stuff my face

Loretta Lost

into the toilet. *What is happening?* I ask myself weakly. *This can't be real. Please let this be a nightmare. I've had so many nightmares about that man—just let this be one more awful dream that I will wake up from at any moment. I just want to be tucked away safe in my little cabin, light years from humanity... any moment now. I'll wake up. Please.*

"I thought my wedding day was supposed to be wonderful," Carmen tells her fiancé softly, "but this is just one headache after another. I just want it to be over so we can be together."

"We'll be happy—soon. I promise you," Grayson says to her gently. He trips over his words slowly and clumsily, with the trepidation of a man who is aware that he is one misstep away from unraveling the fabric of his entire life. "Soon— soon, we'll be family. And nothing—nothing will ever stand between us again. Nothing."

Family. He's going to be family? My stomach lurches again. This is madness. Does he really love her? What is going on? I dig my fingertips into my new head injury, and the pain confirms my darkest dread.

Yes, this is a nightmare. The absolute worst kind of nightmare; real life.

I have to struggle to stay conscious. My mind is still reeling from the shock, and is trying urgently to shut down to shield itself from harm. Sadly, I wish my problems amounted to a simple

CLARITY 2

concussion, but the trauma that's affecting me is much deeper than the mild impact against my skull. I fight to take charge of my own disengaged faculties. Even my body is no longer under my control; I regretfully acknowledge that I am curled up into a tiny ball and shaking like a frightened animal. I realize this is counterproductive and worthless behavior, and I am furious with myself. I try to gather my wits so that I can pick myself off the ground and deal with this situation.

My sister is marrying my rapist, I inform myself. These words feel unreal. They sound ridiculous. The sentence does not pierce the murky depths of my brain, and I try to process the information again. *My sister is about to marry the man who raped me.*

Before I can form a plan of action, I hear the doorknob being jostled violently. My head snaps sharply to the side, and I am stabbed in the heart with multiple daggers of fear.

"Helen?" Grayson says, in a familiar and deceptively humane fashion. "Honey?"

I grind my teeth together. I would have been perfectly happy if I had never heard him speak my name again for the duration of my entire existence. The whole reason I changed my name was to escape the vile memory of him repeating it, over and over in a sadistic song...

"Honey, are you okay in there?" he asks again. "Will you come out so that Carmen doesn't worry about you?"

Pressing my hand against the tub for support, I slowly lift myself off the ground. I find my chest heaving with deep, panting breaths. My tongue circles in the extra bit of sweet saliva that has gathered in my mouth, and all my muscles clench until they grow painfully taut. My body is gearing up for a fight. I don't care if he's a two-hundred-pound football player—or ex-football player. This time, I'm going to tear him limb from limb like a savage beast. I have replayed the event from three years ago in my mind several thousand times. Each time, I do something a little better; I'm a little faster, a little wiser, a little stronger. He will never hurt me again. I won't allow it. But even if he does...

I know one thing for damned certain. There is no way that demon is marrying my sister. He might have gotten the best of me, but I will never allow him to do the same to her. I won't allow him to touch her, ever again. I need to kick this man out of my home, and out of my life for good.

The doorknob jostles again, but this time, it doesn't scare me. I puff out my chest and ball my hands into fists so tightly that my fingernails cut into my palms. How dare he? How dare he violate me and terrorize my family? I remember what my dad said about him being the perfect son-in-law, and my insides shudder with revulsion.

"Excuse me, Miss Winters," says the makeup

CLARITY 2

artist who has been waiting from somewhere distant in Carmen's bedroom. I have to strain to hear her words, because she is speaking softly and the syllables do not perfectly carry through the door. Her voice is impatient and tired. "We haven't finished working on your face."

"Oh, I forgot," Carmen says in horror. "We're running so late! This is awful, Gray. We're probably going to have to delay the ceremony."

"All the guests will wait," Grayson tells her. "You're worth waiting for."

Carmen lets out a shaky little laugh. "At least I cried *before* my makeup was complete..."

"Honey, your bathroom has an entrance to the adjoining room, right?" Grayson asks quietly. "Your sister's old room?"

"Yes," she responds. "Why?"

"Just wait here, love," he tells her with another kiss. "I'll go check on Helen. Why don't you finish getting your makeup done for the wedding photos? Just sit down and relax, honey."

"Gray," Carmen whispers. "Just tell me one thing. Are you sure about me? One hundred percent sure about us?"

"I've never been surer about anything in my life," he tells her. "You need to calm down, love. The day will be over soon, and we can curl up in bed and sleep in tomorrow, for as long as we want. We just have to get through these next couple hours, and satisfy all the family members—we just

Loretta Lost

have to go through the motions for tradition's sake."

"Okay," Carmen says, and there is strength in her voice for the first time in several minutes. "Thank you. You always make me feel better when things get rough."

"That's what I'm here for," he tells her lightly. "I'll be right back."

Now it's time for action. I move to the adjoining door that leads into my bedroom, and I lock it hastily. I wait until I hear Grayson leave Carmen's room, and then I burst through the bathroom door into her room, and push past her. Moving as quickly as I can, I run across the carpeted floor, tripping over beauty supplies and knocking over chairs as I rush to lock her door. I turn back to her in righteous rage and terror, my chest still expanding rapidly with my heavy breathing.

"You can't marry him," I tell her adamantly.

"What?" Carmen says in surprise. "Why? Oh, Helen, you're bleeding..."

"I'm fine," I tell her, gasping for air. "Just listen to me for once in your life. You need to call off this wedding."

"Why are you saying this?" she asks me, her voice wounded. "First Sabrina is a downer, and now you? Why can't anyone be supportive of me?"

"I know him," I tell her, as I continue

CLARITY 2

wheezing. I bend over slightly and place the palms of my hands against my knees to support me. My hands are clammy and cold against my soft and newly shaved legs. The salt in my sweat causes a mild burning sensation against the slightly razor-burned skin of my thighs. I realize that I haven't decided how much I should tell Carmen. It could be very damaging for her to learn the whole truth; that's why I protected her from it in the first place. But now? Now that she has fallen in love with him, I'm not sure what might be the proper protocol for this situation. "I know him from school, Carmen. He's a criminal. He's done horrible things."

"Stop," she hisses sharply. "Just stop. I don't want to hear about it."

I frown at the tone in her voice. "You're about to marry this man, and you don't even know who he is! He's going to ruin your life. Call it off. Please call it off, for your own sake."

"I can't believe you," Carmen whispers. "Why would you do this to me? You're supposed to be happy for me."

"I would be happy if it were almost anyone else," I say in a deadly serious voice. "Carmen. You need to call it off."

"Why?" she demands.

How can I say anything without hurting her? I part my lips, trying to think of the right words. I can't just blurt out the truth, can I? No. It would devastate her. She would be upset enough about her cancelled wedding, and the embarrassment to all her friends and relatives—but then she would also need to deal with what happened to me. It would be too much for her to handle in this moment. "He's going to hurt you," I tell her, closing my eyes. "He's not a good person."

"Look," Carmen snaps in annoyance. "We're all flawed in some way. We all make mistakes. If I spend my life waiting for the perfect man, I'll be waiting forever."

"Flawed? He's not just flawed. He's a fucking monster."

"Helen!" she says in shock. "You're talking about the man who's going to be my husband in a few hours."

The makeup artist clears her throat. "We really need to get the bride's face ready for photos... unless you're calling the wedding off?"

"I'm not!" Carmen declares. "I'm getting married."

Just then, to add another horrible element to the chaos, Grayson tries to re-enter the room. He turns the knob, and finds that it has been locked. "Carmen?" he says in confusion as he fiddles with it. "Will you let me in?"

In a panic, I move over to the dresser where I had left my phone. I pick it up with shaking hands, and hastily shove the single circular button. "Dial 911," I speak into the phone anxiously.

CLARITY 2

"What the fuck are you doing?!" Carmen asks, leaping forward and grabbing the phone from my hands.

"Calling 91..."

She interrupts my phone call before it can be completed, but places a hand on my arm. "Helen," she says quietly. "Did he really do something worthy of arrest?"

"Yes," I say, swallowing nervously. "Give me my phone. I'm calling the cops."

"Please don't," Carmen begs. "If you destroy him, you'll destroy me. Our lives are already so intertwined. We are practically married as it is! Anything that happened? Anything he did? It's a family matter now. We'll deal with it right here, between us."

"You're being so weak right now," I say to her in surprise. "This isn't like you. Why would you ignore important information and go ahead with a decision that can only end in tears?"

"Is everything okay in there?" Grayson calls from outside the room, jostling the doorknob.

Carmen takes a deep breath. "Listen to me, Helen. I'm not young and idealistic anymore. I've grown up, and I know that I need to make compromises."

"You can't compromise on *this!*" I hiss. "You can't compromise on your safety!"

There is the sound of an item being tossed across the room and I flinch when it smashes into the wall. Carmen has snapped. I just hope it was a random beauty implement that fell victim to her rage, and not my cell phone.

"You weren't here for me!" Carmen screams. "You were gone! Do you know how much you hurt me? Who the hell do you think you are? You left! You'll probably just leave again tomorrow. This family obviously means nothing to you. *I* mean nothing to you!"

I can feel her breath on my face as she moves close to me so that her yelling can pierce my ears more painfully. I can also feel the eyes of the makeup artist on us. I am embarrassed as I wonder what she thinks of us—is this normal wedding behavior? It might be. There is also a hair stylist in the room, but it sounds like she is sitting and typing on her phone, and not bothered. There was another makeup artist in the room earlier, but it seems like she might have left when I was helping Carmen put on her dress. My sister is still screaming at me, and I wince as her already shrill voice increases by a few decibels.

"Don't think you can come in here at the last minute and stick your nose in my business! Don't think you can order me around and interfere with my choices like you give a fuck! Grayson has been there for me every single day, for years. I'm not throwing that away because you're a bitter little bitch."

I lift my hands into the air, and they float

CLARITY 2

there in confusion and bewilderment. Although I know that my leaving was justified, I still feel terrible. I wonder for a moment if Grayson really can be healthier for my sister than I am. Is it possible that he is trying to be good to her to atone for what he did to me? Is this all part of some kind of twisted plan for redemption? I can't imagine what an appalled and horrified look I must have on my face, because Carmen gasps and sobs.

"I'm sorry, Helen," she says, placing my phone against the palm of my hand. I am relieved to feel that it is in one piece. "Just—stay out of it, okay? Grayson is my guy. I accept him for who he is. Please understand that."

"But Carm—" I begin in protest.

"No. I won't listen to any more of it. This is a seriously big and empty house, and I can't be alone here for another day. The silence is deafening. Every little noise, every creak and sigh drives me insane." She pauses. "But worse than that... my whole *life* is a big and empty house that people just walk in and out of as they please. No one stays with me. I need to start building a home where I feel welcome and wanted. I need to start building the foundation of my future. You understand that, don't you? I'm much older than you, Helen. I can't play games or life will pass me by. It's time for me to move forward. Grayson treats me well. This is what I need."

I stand in stunned silence as I allow her

words to sink into my brain.

"Look. I need to get my makeup on," Carmen says softly. "Can you please just be happy for me, little sister? Can you please just be supportive?"

"Carmen!" Grayson shouts from outside the room. "Please open the door, love. What's going on? You never lock your door—I'm getting worried."

"Excuse me," Carmen says to me as she moves toward the door.

My legs feel like lead, and I remain rooted to the spot. Only when I hear Carmen unlocking her door do I realize that Grayson is about to enter the room. The thought of coming face-to-face with him sends a violent shiver through my body. There is a sharp pain in my shoulders and neck where all my muscles are clenched and bunched up tightly. For a moment, it is difficult to force myself to move, because my brain seems disconnected from the rest of me.

But then I hear his footstep.

I suddenly spring into motion as though he has set the ground beneath me on fire with his presence in the room. I can't bear the thought of him looking at me, and I hope I can move quickly enough that he barely glimpses a flash of my hair disappearing. I find myself bolting back into the bathroom and ripping the door open to my bedroom. I need locked doors between me and that

CLARITY 2

man. As many locked doors as possible. I know that they don't offer complete protection, but they certainly help my anxiety. Once I have successfully barricaded every entrance, I move to grasp the post of my bed.

I close my eyes and press my forehead against the cool varnished wood.

With a sigh, I non-too-gently thump my forehead against the bedpost. "Why," I grumble to myself blankly. "Why. Why. Why." I don't even have the energy to speak the word in the form of a question. The universe isn't going to answer me; it doesn't need to justify itself. It's just having fun. I don't think it even cares whether that fun is at my expense.

I fight the urge to lift my fist into the air and give God an excellent view of my middle finger. I have never been very religious, but for one single moment, I am almost completely certain that there must be one single, sick bastard responsible for this. I fight the urge to call him names, or ask *why* a few more dozen times.

I fight the urge to throw myself out of the second-story window.

An object vibrating in my hand startles me, and I jump and reflexively toss it away, as though stung by an insect. I then register the sound of ringing. My mind has been spinning so wildly that it takes me a moment to process that I am receiving a phone call. *Why?* I inwardly ask myself

Loretta Lost

again. Even this phone call is too much to bear. I went so many days with zero contact from the outside world—so many weeks and months, with only the necessary communication for my job. Now, in one day, I am suddenly popular. I suddenly have to talk to people and touch them, and answer phone calls. It's too much. It's terrifying. But my phone continues to ring.

I fumble for the small device that I had dropped on my bed. Collecting it, I quickly answer it in a curt and businesslike voice. "Yes?"

"Helen! Sorry to call again so soon," says the voice on the other end of the phone. "I am having a bit of a wardrobe crisis—I don't go to special events very often. I thought I'd just ask to make sure. Do I wear a bow tie or a normal tie?"

My nose wrinkles with irritation. "Don't bother," I say in a dry tone.

"What?" Liam asks, sounding somewhat surprised. "What's going on? Just a few minutes ago, you said..."

"Forget what I said!" I snap harshly. My entire face contorts with heat and rage. "Just—forget it. Don't bother coming here."

"Did something happen, Helen?" He pauses, and his voice sounds almost hurt. "You're acting different. I thought we were going to have fun with this fake-date thing. Is everything okay?"

"Everything's fine," I tell him quietly, "but it looks like my sister isn't getting married after all."

CLARITY 2

"What? But she said..."

"I don't care what she said," I hiss into the phone. "I'm going to stop this fucking wedding."

And with that proclamation, I hung up the phone. I stand victorious in my resolve for a moment, breathing heavily in fury. Then it occurs to me that I have no clue in hell how I'm going to stop this wedding without trampling on my sister's heart, and destroying the hopes of my fragile father. Feeling suddenly drained of my strength, I move over to collapse facedown onto my bed. My face sinks into the fluffy duvet atop the lovely farmhouse bed that I haven't slept on in three years. It is much larger and softer than the tiny, hard cot I slept on back in my cabin, but in this moment, I cannot appreciate the luxury. I would gladly lie down on anything; even a bed of dirt in the slums of India, if it meant I would be far away from this house and *him*.

"Why," I mutter again into the pillow as my makeup surely gets smudged all over the fabric. I can't seem to form any other utterance. "Why."

Chapter Two

I'm not sure how long I've been lying flat on my face before I can no longer stand the inertia. I have been running dozens of possible scenarios through my mind, and trying to choose the best course of action. I have been hovering in a strange meditative state somewhere between wakefulness and slumber, and it has been calm and serene. I can hear people rushing about the corridor outside my room, but I have been able to block it out and listen only to my inner voice. I have been able to reach inside myself and grasp a few morsels of wisdom and patience, to help me combat my overpowering anger and fear.

I need to tread carefully.

With a few words, I have the power to drop an avalanche on my sister's head. It's the right thing to do, but I shouldn't be hasty and careless. I need to be graceful and delicate in my delivery, or I could hurt her just as much as Grayson. The fact is that Carmen doesn't trust me. She sees me as an outsider, or even an enemy, and anything I can say

CLARITY 2

or do to protect her will seem malicious and spiteful. I hear a female voice in the corridor, and I recognize it as an older family member.

Rising to my feet, I head to my bedroom door and unlock it before bravely swinging it wide open.

"There you are, child!" says the old woman's voice. "Oh, look at you, Helen. You're absolutely darling in that gown! You look just like your mother. I've been sent to collect you. It's time for the family wedding photos!"

"Aunt Edna," I say firmly. "My sister is making a huge mistake. She can't marry Grayson."

"What do you mean, dear?" The older woman chuckles softly. "Why, I've never met a finer boy than that Grayson. Your sister sure got lucky and picked a good one!"

"No. She didn't." I grip the door frame tightly, and almost expect the wood to shatter under my fingers. "Aunt Edna. You have to talk to my dad and get him to convince Carmen to stop the wedding. I have evidence that Grayson is... only after our family's money."

"Good gracious, child!" Aunt Edna scoffs. "I hardly think that's true. From what your father tells me, that boy single-handedly saved the family fortune! Grayson helped your dad make hundreds of thousands of dollars from investments in only a few short years. He's the only reason you could keep the house!"

Loretta Lost

"But Aunt Edna," I say sharply. "I have reason to believe..."

"Rubbish! Stop this nonsense immediately. Grayson is a lovely young man, and your sister is going to be just fine." Aunt Edna reaches out to slip her hand under my arm and guide me into the hallway. "Besides," she says in a conspiratorial whisper, "they have a pre-nup. My husband saw to that, and it's iron-clad. If something goes wrong and your sister needs to divorce him, he doesn't get anything! So, you can stop worrying, dear."

I groan and stiffly follow the woman as she guides me through the hallway.

"Really, I understand your concerns," Aunt Edna chatters on. "Why, when my daughter got married, I was in such a fright..."

"Excuse me, Aunt Edna," I say, pulling my arm away and trying to escape as gently as possible. "I forgot something important that I need to do." I slip away from her and move toward the staircase. The scent of the flowers decorating the main foyer fills my nostrils again, but it does not enchant me the way it did before. I don't have even a millisecond to pause and appreciate them. There are dozens of voices in the house, and I realize that many of the guests have begun to arrive.

I should not have waited so long. By being depressed and indecisive, I have probably made cancelling the wedding far more painful to

CLARITY 2

Carmen. People start to greet me as I descend the staircase, and dive into the confusing sea of voices. My head begins to spin a bit, as I try to move through the crowd without colliding with anyone.

"Helen, dear! Oh, you've grown so big, sweetie!" says a deep woman's voice.

"Thank you," I mumble with a nod as I slip past her.

"Well, if it isn't little Helen Keller," says a cheerful man's voice—I think it's one of our uncles. "I heard you've written some books! Boy, you never cease to amaze me. Being blind never slowed you down, kiddo!"

"Thanks," I say again as I move past him. I am startled when I feel a large hand on my shoulder. I jump and rip my body away from the physical contact.

"Cousin Helen? Holy shit! The last time I saw you, we were both four feet tall. You turned out a lot prettier than I expected."

"Thanks," I say again as try to move away, but the male voice follows me.

"Can you believe Carmen's getting married? She's such an airhead. I always figured she'd just spend her life moving from random dude to random dude. But I was sure that *you'd* settle down and get married. You've always been the serious one!"

"Excuse me," I say, trying to pull away from him.

Loretta Lost

"Hey, you don't recognize my voice?" he asks, sounding hurt. He grabs my elbow gently. "It's Cousin Charlie! Remember, we shared our first kiss in the attic when we were ten?"

"Sure. Great to see you," I say as I remove his hand from my arm. I deftly maneuver around him so that I can escape. I cringe a little in memory of the kid that Carmen and I had dubbed Creepy Cousin Charlie—yet there is a bit of wistfulness in my expression. I long for the days when our biggest problem was an awkward young boy who wanted to play spin the bottle a little too often. Now that we are larger, it seems that the dangers have grown along with us, escalating from tiny annoyances into real threats.

I push these thoughts aside as I continue to navigate through the crowd, heading for my father's library. Like me, he has never enjoyed crowds very much, and chances are that he will be locked away in the quiet privacy of his study until it is absolutely necessary to socialize. A few more people try to accost me for conversation as I move through the foyer, but I excuse myself. I accidentally bump into a fat woman's squishy body, and quickly apologize and step away. I wince in embarrassment and aversion. Every time I come into contact with another person, my insides quake in momentary terror. But it's unavoidable.

Trying to move gracefully through a crowded room when you're blind is kind of like dancing in

CLARITY 2

a swarm of bees and expecting not to get stung.

After great effort, I finally arrive at the doors to my father's library. I am pleased to see that they are closed, and I quickly slide them open and slip inside. Tugging the doors closed behind me, I release a sigh of relief as the noise from all the wedding guests is instantly—but not completely—muffled. I feel as though I have placed all the bees into a jar and fastened the lid tightly closed; for a moment, they are no longer an issue. I hear breathing in the room with me, and I am glad to know my father is in his library, as always. Now I can finally discuss the situation and stop this wedding.

"Dad?" I say with determination. "I need to talk to you about Grayson."

There is a silence. "No," he responds quietly. "You don't need to say anything to anyone."

My heart feels like it has been jabbed with a taser. For a moment, my insides are paralyzed. It is *his* voice—I am in the room alone with *him*. I am too frozen to escape before I feel two hands circling around my waist.

"Helen," he whispers. "I thought I'd never see you again."

I am torn between wanting to run, scream, lash out and hurt him, or say something profound and wise that will fix everything. However, my mind can't work quickly enough to decide what to do, or what I could possibly say, and I end up immobilized in anxiety.

I can feel his face descending close to mine. The bristles of his chin scratch against my cheek as he puts his lips close to my ear. His breath tickles the tiny wisps of wayward curls framing my face.

"You shouldn't have come back here," he tells me. "I'm never going to be able to let you go. Those mesmerizing amber eyes of yours—it's such a pity they're useless."

Finally, I am so appalled that I am able to break through my barrier of fear and push him away. "Don't touch me," I hiss, and my voice is filled with snakelike venom. "I don't know how you weaseled your way into my home and into my family, but you are *not* going to marry my sister."

He laughs softly. "You're delightful when you're pissed. Unfortunately, I *am* going to marry Carmen. We've been together for years—and in case you haven't noticed, your entire extended family is already here, eagerly anticipating the wedding."

"I don't give a flying fuck," I tell him. "They don't know who you are and what you did to me. I'm giving you one chance, Grayson. Call the wedding off and tell them you changed your mind. Or I'm going to expose you and send you to jail."

"That's the first time I've heard you say my name," he says in wonder. "It sounds so refined coming from your lips. Say it again."

I close my eyes briefly. This man is beyond

CLARITY 2

infuriating. I need to find a way to overpower him with my words. "Three years ago, you raped me. All I need to do is tell someone that it was you..."

"How do you know it was me?" he asks. "You have no idea what I look like."

My face twists into a scowl. "No one is going to doubt my judgment."

"Maybe I'm not who you think I am. Did you ever think that maybe you have me confused with someone else?" He moves close to me again, and reaches for me. I back away, but he grabs me and pins me to the door beside the wall. "You can't positively identify me. You have no evidence."

"That's where you're wrong," I tell him quietly as I peel his hands off my body. "After you beat me unconscious and I woke up, I immediately filed a police report. They checked me out and created a rape kit." This time, I'm the one stepping forward and lifting my chin to put my face close to his. I need to be as intimidating as possible. I need to show that I won't back down. "If I ask them to reopen my case and test my rape kit, whose DNA do you think they'll find? If you don't call off the wedding *now,* then we'll find out. I wager you won't be too happy with the results."

There is a moment of stillness as he considers this. I hold my breath, thinking that I might be victorious. Did my threat work? Can he tell I'm bluffing? Of course, there is no rape kit. I was so depressed that I was unable to file a police

Loretta Lost

report or do much of anything after the event. I only had the presence of mind to call our family doctor, Leslie Howard, and have her bring me emergency contraception. I listen to the silence, trying to figure out what Grayson is thinking. Does he believe me? This is my trump card; if this doesn't work, I have no other ideas.

I hear a little metallic click, and I feel a cold nozzle pressed against my forehead, between my eyes.

"Do you know what this is, Helen?" he asks me softly.

My heart starts racing. Is he going to kill me? Right here in my father's library? I am so terrified that I can't reassure myself with the reminder that there are dozens of people just outside the door who might hear the shot. I know what this man is capable of—but I don't know how smart he is.

"This is a gun. Don't worry, sweet thing. I'm not going to put a bullet in your head." He slowly drags the nozzle of the gun down along my nose, and roughly over my lips. He rakes the gun down over my neck and collarbone, until he slides it into place over my heart. The gun lingers there for a moment, between my breasts. "I'm not going to put a bullet in your chest, either. But let me tell you this..."

He lowers his voice to a deathly whisper as he lifts a hand to cup my cheek. "If you tell anyone *anything* about what happened three years ago—or

CLARITY 2

if you do *anything* to jeopardize my marriage to your sister—I will kill Carmen. I will put a bullet in your sister's head. I will put a bullet in your sister's chest. And then I'll shoot myself. I love your sister more than I've ever loved another human being. If you take that away from me—if you take that away from *us*—you might as well be killing us both."

All the energy drains from my body. I am defeated.

"Do you understand me?" he demands, shoving the gun forward painfully so that it digs into my chest and pushes me slightly off balance. "If you don't keep your mouth shut, I'll kill Carmen. Why are you just standing there? Can you hear me? Nod if you understand."

Very slowly, and with great effort, I force myself to nod.

"Great. But don't worry," he says gently, removing the gun from my chest and returning it to his blazer. "There's no need to be jealous. I still have plenty of love to give to you."

"Go to hell," I whisper.

He laughs and grasps the back of my head, leaning down to force a kiss against my lips.

I am stupefied and speechless by his gall. Thankfully, he doesn't try to do more than this, because I no longer have the strength to fight. I feel like the blood has left my veins and been replaced by empty air. I won't risk my sister's life, and he must know that. He has won. When he moves away, I hear him wiping his mouth with his sleeve to remove any telltale traces of lipstick. For a brief moment, a spark of fury fills me with fire. I consider tackling him and trying to steal the gun away from him—maybe I could shoot *him* in the chest. But the thought disappears as soon as it comes. Even if my limbs didn't feel lifeless and weak, I am not sure I could be capable of such cruelty. I am not even sure if he deserves such treatment. After all—he did not take my life. It would be unfair to take his.

"It's been a pleasure catching up with you," Grayson says as he walks to the library doors. "But I've got to get back to my wedding. Haven't you heard? It's the most important day of my life." He pushes open the sliding doors and moves back into the foyer. There are joyous sounds of welcoming as the other guests greet him with good cheer and claps on the back.

I am left standing alone and staring into my familiar nothingness.

Chapter Three

"Here she is! I've found her!" announces a female voice loudly. I recognize it as Carmen's bridesmaid Sabrina. She rushes into the library and grabs my arm. "Where have you been? You missed the photos!"

I am still slightly in a daze as I allow her to pull me out into the cacophony of the crowd.

"Oh, Helen," Carmen says in disappointment. "You forgot your shoes in my bedroom. I've been looking for you. I can't believe you're walking around barefoot when all the guests are here. Stop being ridiculous."

I feel a pair of high-heeled shoes thrust against my chest, and I lift my arms to grasp them. The sharp heels poking into my skin do not bother me nearly as much as the cold metal cylinder just did.

"They're such lovely shoes," Sabrina says with a sigh. "Most women make their bridesmaids look hideous, but Carmen really picked out exquisite clothes for us. It's too bad you can't see the shoes, Helen."

I can hardly be bothered to care, but I try to force myself to go through the motions. Skimming my fingers over the satiny shoes, I feel some kind of jeweled embellishment on the front. They have a peep toe and a small kitten heel. I don't know why I bothered to examine the shoes, because I can't even try to make my face seem interested.

"Put them on!" Carmen urges. "Today, you are merely one of my decorations. You have to dress up exactly as the bride wishes, and I am *not* doing a barefoot-on-the-beach style wedding."

The excitement in her voice makes me feel ill. All I can think about is the sensation of the gun nozzle pressed against my chest. *If you don't keep your mouth shut, I'll kill Carmen.* How can she be so happy, when just a few minutes before, her fiancé threatened to kill her? She is so innocent— and there is nothing I can do to inform her. My trump card failed. I have no other ideas. Unless I can think of something really ingenious, it looks like Grayson is going to get his way.

"Put on the shoes, Helen," Carmen commands in an annoyed voice.

"Fine," I say miserably. I allow both of the shoes to clatter from my arms to the ground. I then use my toe to poke around, searching for the entrance to the footwear. As I do this, I try to maintain my balance on one foot, but I'm sure I

CLARITY 2

look wobbly and pathetic—which is precisely the way I feel. When I finally discover a shoe and try to insert my foot, of course, it happens to be the wrong shoe. I utter a very unladylike curse.

"Allow me to help you with that," says a deep male voice. I am not sure who it is, but I am comforted by the fact that it is not Grayson. At this moment, any other man is a potential ally. I can feel that he has crouched down before me, for he gently takes my wrist and positions it on his shoulder so that I have some support. I don't even have the energy to protest, for I feel that I might actually fall over without his assistance. I am so discombobulated. His hand carefully encircles my foot and guides it into the correct high-heeled shoe. I am expecting him to immediately release me and disappear, but he holds my foot there for a moment, until I feel steady again. After a second, he picks up the other shoe and helps me place my second foot into the encasement.

"Thank you," I whisper, pleasantly surprised by the tenderness of his touch.

"Not a problem," he says kindly.

His voice is somehow calming to me. There are dozens of voices all around me in the crowded foyer, but his is soft and serene. When he speaks, I feel like I've discovered the solitary safe place in the middle of a raging storm. There is shelter and protection in his quiet strength.

"Helen? What's wrong?" he asks me with

Loretta Lost

concern. He reaches up to clasp my hand as it rests on his shoulder. "You're so pale—like you've seen a ghost."

I am suddenly even more confused. First of all, I am stricken by the fact that I am supposed to know this man. Is he one of our family members? Another distant cousin? I search my memory for his voice, but I am drawing a blank. Second of all, how does he know me so well? How can he see that I am pale and shaken, while my own sister is oblivious to this?

"Whoa," Carmen says with a strange tone in her voice. "Who's Prince Charming over here with the glass slippers?"

The man on the ground laughs lightly. He removes my hand from his shoulder as he rises to his feet. "That's right. We haven't been introduced. Helen, will you do the honors?"

I am worried that my face betrays how clueless I am. Luckily, I am saved by my father's booming voice.

"Ladies! How are we all doing over here?" my father asks happily. "I think it was a splendid idea to serve cocktails to the guests before the wedding, Carmen. Everyone is in such good spirits—pardon the pun!"

"Oh, Dad," Carmen says with a giggle. "How much have you had to drink?"

"Just enough, darling. Just enough."

There is a twinkle in his tone, as though he

CLARITY 2

might be winking at my sister. His voice makes me feel much better, too. I wish I could take him aside and tell him what I know, but I can no longer try to save the day with the grave threat looming over my head.

"Oh, there you are, my good fellow!" my father says, and his voice is directed at the person standing next to me—the man who helped with my shoes. "I just ran into this fine gentleman a few minutes ago. Imagine my surprise when he introduced himself as my daughter's boyfriend!"

For a moment, I am bewildered. Carmen has a boyfriend? In addition to Grayson? Does Grayson know about this? I immediately start to hope that there's a chance for the wedding to be halted by other complications. My mind runs away with me, and I imagine a brave prince coming to the rescue and beating the shit out of Grayson.

"Oh my god," Carmen says in astonishment. "*This* is Liam? *This* is Helen's boyfriend?"

I am stunned by this information and deeply embarrassed that I *forgot* the voice of my supposed suitor. I am shocked that he is here at all, considering I told him not to come.

"That's right," Liam says, placing a hand affectionately on my back. "We've only been dating for a year, but it's been the best year of my life. Helen is an incredible woman."

The palm of his hand is warm against my spine, and I can feel my cheeks growing red. This is so absurd and embarrassing. I can't remember why I decided to do this. Now, after all that's happened, it feels so pointless and bizarre that I ever asked Liam to be my fake date to this wedding. How stupid was that? Why did I even care about such trivial bullshit? My sister's life is on the line, and I feel like a fool. I can't believe I thought it would be fun. Still... I can't help but be glad that Liam is here. His presence is somehow reassuring.

"Holy shit!" Carmen exclaims in amazement. "Helen, you didn't tell me that he's gorgeous!"

"Yeah," Sabrina adds solemnly. "Wow."

I shrug to hide my mortification and annoyance. "How could I have told you that? I have no idea what he looks like."

"Well, you could have told me more about what he *feels* like," Carmen says with an audacious giggle.

"Oh my god," I mutter softly, turning to Liam. "I'm so sorry about this."

"It's quite alright," he says with amusement.

Sabrina clucks her tongue in disapproval. "Helen, didn't you know you that you're not supposed to bring a man to the wedding who's more handsome than the groom? It's bad etiquette!"

"Uhh." I don't know how to respond to their flattery, and my cheeks flush even darker. I'm not sure whether I'm more embarrassed at being the

CLARITY 2

center of attention, at the fact that dating Liam is a lie, or at the fact that it is now confirmed that he's incredibly attractive, which makes me feel a little uneasy. If I was going to create a convincing lie, I probably should have chosen someone plain and forgettable, who was a little more in my league.

"Alright, children. That's enough of teasing poor Helen," my father says with a laugh. "She's red as a beet! Don't we have a wedding to get started? It's about ten minutes to show time! Grayson's standing over there and looking very impatient."

"Oh, let him wait," Carmen says flippantly. "He's been pressuring me to marry him for years. I'm sure he can handle another ten minutes of waiting."

"That's your fiancé?" Liam asks. "He seems a bit... angry."

"No, no," my father answers. "I'm sure it's just the wedding-day pressure getting to him. It's a lot of stress. I can assure you that Grayson is the nicest guy in the world."

I can't keep a small grunt of derision from leaving my throat. It goes undetected by everyone around me, except for Liam. His hand on my back moves up and down in a soothing manner. I am surprised at how attentive and intuitive he is.

"Well, I suppose we might as well start getting ready," Carmen grumbles. "Let's usher everyone to their seats."

Loretta Lost

A moment later, Carmen, Sabrina, and my father are gone. The wedding is about to begin, and it will proceed as planned. I have failed in trying to stop it. Unless...

"Hey. What's wrong?" Liam asks me again. "Come on, Helen. Talk to me. There's this look on your face, like you just stepped on a landmine."

"I did," I say softly. Then I turn to him with a frown. "What are you doing here anyway? I told you not to come."

"You sounded distraught," he tells me. "I don't know—I was worried. What's the matter? Something is bothering you; I can see that. When I walked in, you were as white as death."

"Liam," I say quietly, moving close to him. My eyebrows knit together in consternation. "Thank you for coming. I just..."

A passionate female voice interrupts me. "Hellie! Can I speak to you in private for a moment?"

"Carm?" I say in surprise. "Uh, sure."

"I hope you don't mind if I steal her, Liam." Carmen says this as she slips her hand on my arm, already prepared to drag me away. I am a bit disappointed at the interruption, but I appreciate one final chance to talk to my sister.

"Not a problem," Liam says. "I think I see someone I know—Dr. Leslie Howard. I'll go chat with her in the meantime."

"Great!" Carmen chimes in as she leads me

CLARITY 2

back into the privacy of the library.

I am nervous that Grayson might be suspicious of me speaking to Carmen alone—if he can see us. And I'm sure he's keeping an eye on me. Nonetheless, I can't waste this opportunity to tell her. *Should* I tell her? Is it worth the risk? I am startled out of my thoughts when Carmen pulls me into a hug.

"I just wanted to congratulate you, Helen. I know we were joking around about Liam's hotness a few minutes ago, but I wanted to be serious for a sec. He seems so sweet and loving. The way he helped you with your shoes! What a gentleman. You two seem perfect for each other, and I'm so happy for you. I think this is the first time I've ever seen you with a guy—the first time you ever brought someone home. Gosh... he's your first *real* boyfriend!"

I flinch at her words. He's certainly my first fake boyfriend.

"My little sister's growing up," Carmen says affectionately. "Sorry. I'm just so emotional today. This is so special."

"Yeah," I mutter in frustration. "So special."

"Honestly, I'm jealous," Carmen whispers. "Grayson is pretty cute, but Liam is a *stud*. Gosh. Aren't you glad you wore the thong?"

"No. Not really."

"Why can't you be a little excited with me, Helen? Seriously. I'm just trying to enjoy the moment and bask in our happiness." She moves over to the library doors to peer out at the crowd with a sigh. "I mean, if only you could *see* this adorable man who's all yours..."

"There has to be more to a man than his appearance," I tell her briskly. "I really don't care what he looks like."

"But doesn't it help to know that... oh. Hey, Helen?" Carmen pauses and hesitates. "How well does your boyfriend know Dr. Howard? They seem pretty close."

"Liam and Leslie?" I ask in surprise. I immediately frown at how nice their names sound together. "Well... they're colleagues."

"They seem like a little more than just colleagues to me," Carmen observes.

"What do you mean?" I ask, without really wanting to. It's none of my concern.

"Well, he just hugged her and she kissed him on the cheek. They seem really affectionate."

"Oh," I say in disappointment. "I thought she was close to Mom's age?"

"Yes," Carmen responds slowly, "but she's very well put-together. I'm almost positive she's had some work done. She might be a bit of a... cougar."

I make a face. This upsets me. Why does it upset me? Liam isn't actually my boyfriend, and I don't actually care if he has something going on with an older woman. How do I even have the

CLARITY 2

ability to care about anything other than the situation with Grayson? I am shocked at my endless capacity to be even more hurt and upset that I was a few minutes before.

"Maybe I'm wrong," Carmen says. "I shouldn't judge things so easily. You know how I always jump to conclusions and make the wrong assump..."

"Grayson is a rapist."

My sister abruptly stops her prattling. There is a silence in the library. I did not mean to say this, but I was unable to keep it inside any longer. I immediately regret having spoken, and wished I had delivered the information in a different way. I just didn't have any time to think. It needed to be done *now*. Finally, when Carmen speaks, her voice is a tiny whisper.

"I know."

"What?" I say in horror. "You know? You *know?*"

"Yes. Helen..."

"Then why the hell are you marrying him?"

"It's not what you think." She takes several deep breaths and pulls me further into the shadows of the library. "He—he has a problem. I've done some research... psychological research. I think it's like a mental illness. Or just part of who he is. Either way, I accept this about him."

"Carmen, are you insane?" I struggle to keep my voice down because I'm moments away from screaming at her or grabbing and shaking her. "Has he ever hurt you?"

"Well, he's aggressive sometimes. He's never hit me, but sometimes..."

"Sometimes what?" I demand.

She hesitates. "If I'm sleeping, or if I'm not feeling well. Like, if I'm on my period, and I have cramps... he will force himself on me." She gulps loudly. "Look, it's only been a few times, and he's always really apologetic afterward. We've gone to counseling. I swear, it's just this one thing—he's a great guy in every other way."

I feel so sick at hearing this. "You can't marry him."

"I have to. I love him. Please... please respect my decision, Helen. I know it seems messed up— but even though he hurts me, I know he doesn't *really* mean to hurt me. I've talked to him about it. I don't know what it is, but he has some kind of issue. He can't control himself sometimes."

"There are no excuses. If you marry him, it will only get worse."

"It's just sex, Helen! He's been nothing but supportive and openhearted in other ways. In every other way."

"Carmen, I can't believe what you're saying. You can't do this." I am losing my temper and trying to be calm, but I find myself grabbing her shoulders. "Did you know that in a lot of countries, it's *legal* to rape your wife? Even here, it's only

CLARITY 2

been taken seriously in recent history. Traditionally, wives are supposed to be submissive to their husband, and that attitude is still a huge part of our culture. You can't agree to a life with someone who doesn't respect you."

"He respects me," Carmen insists. Her body trembles under my hands as though she is silently crying. "I swear to you, Helen. He respects me."

"Are you insane?" I shake my head in disbelief. "You're throwing away your freedom and the sanctity of your body. You're subjugating yourself to abuse! And you're *defending* him?"

"Yes, I'm defending him!" Carmen says sharply. "Believe it or not, I've had worse boyfriends. I've dated guys who tried to interfere with my school or my career. I dated guys that were jerks to Dad. I dated guys who were emotionally abusive and got drunk on an almost nightly basis, and said the cruelest things to me. I dated guys who drove recklessly and got into several accidents with me in the vehicle. I dated guys with drug problems who tried to get me addicted and waste our days away being high. Yes, I'm sad and pathetic. But Grayson is the best guy I've ever met. He's the best guy I've ever been with, even with his flaws. And I'm marrying him!"

"Are you fucking kidding me right now?" I ask her in shock. "He just threatened to kill you if I told you what I know about him."

"He doesn't mean it," Carmen says tearfully.

Loretta Lost

"Trust me, he's just using scare tactics—he really doesn't mean it, and he would never hurt me."

"You just told me he *raped* you."

"Yes, but... it's not complete rape. I want to have sex with him most of the time. Look, it's just a super small issue, Hellie. It's my fault too. If I had just been in the mood..."

"Oh my god," I say in disbelief and horror. "Who *are* you? What the fuck are you even saying right now? I thought my big sister was strong and brave. I thought she didn't take crap from anyone."

"I've changed since we lost Mom," Carmen tells me. "Now... I'd rather take a little crap from people than be completely alone forever."

"I won't let you," I tell her firmly. "You won't be alone, but you can't marry *him.* He's an animal. You deserve better!"

Carmen sighs. "I'm too tired, Helen. I'm too old to meet someone new and get to know him all over again. I've been with Grayson for a long time, and we are good together. I don't want to start all over again with someone else who could be even worse once I discover who he really is—it takes *years* to really figure a person out."

"You haven't even figured Grayson out!" I accuse her. "You don't even know how foul he is. Let me tell you what he did. Maybe if you know that you're not the only one he's hurt, you'll understand and take action."

"Helen," she says brokenly. "Don't."

CLARITY 2

"Do you remember when I came home with all those bruises? When I said I was mugged?"

"No!" Carmen almost shouts at me. Her words are laced with small, heart-wrenching sobs. "Please. Stop. I can't know this. Don't say another word. I'm fucked, Helen. I'm so fucked."

"You need to hear this," I insist. "He's the one who..."

"Helen, I'm three months pregnant."

The words get caught in my throat. I find myself rendered speechless.

"Whatever he's done?" Carmen whispers. "I can't know. He's the father of my baby. I can't... I can't back out of this now. I need him. I want my baby to grow up with a good father, like we did."

My hands fall to my side, quite limp and robbed of their fire. I lower my head.

"I need to sit down," Carmen says as she moves over to a chair in the corner of the library. She takes several deep breaths. "So now you know. I think it's why I've been so hormonal," she says with a small, miserable laugh. "It's why I've been crying so easily. Oh, and of course, it's why I was throwing up earlier. Why I had Tylenol instead of Advil, and no champagne while getting ready..."

"Is it also why you've lost your mind?" I ask her quietly.

"Yes," she answers. "I know that Grayson will be a good father. I don't care if he hurts me sometimes. That's the price I'm willing to pay to have the security of a good man and a strong family. As long as he takes care of my baby, nothing else matters."

I close my eyes, trying to un-see the horrible images in my mind. In this moment, I see too much. I vividly remember calling Dr. Howard to get me the morning-after pill when this happened to me. She tried to get me to file a police report and do a rape kit, but I just wanted to put the attack behind me. Now, I wish I had. If only I had known that my rapist wouldn't stop there, and that he would take things even further and hurt my sister? Or any other woman?

I was being selfish. I just wanted to run away to save myself, when I should have stayed to fight. This is all my fault. And now, this man has raped my sister into fathering my niece or nephew. He's trapped her. Emotionally, financially, and probably in dozens of ways I can't begin to guess, he's made her his prisoner.

"What if he hurts your child?" I ask her softly. "What if it's a girl, and when she's a teenager..."

"No. Don't even say that," Carmen tells me. "He wouldn't—"

Music starts playing from the ballroom where the wedding is being held. It's the music meant to announce Carmen's entrance into the room.

CLARITY 2

"Oh god," she says quietly, leaping up from her chair. "Oh god. How's my makeup? Shit, you can't even see my makeup. Oh god."

"Your makeup is the least of your worries," I tell her dryly.

"Look, Helen. I've made my choice. Maybe it's a bad choice, but I can't change my mind now. It's too late. I'm in too deep." She sniffles and wipes her face. "I have to go now. I love him, and I know he'll be a good father. I just want to present a good image to everyone else. I want to seem strong and happy to all our family and friends. Who cares if I have some private issues that bother me behind closed doors? Everyone has skeletons in their closets. I'm going to head inside now."

"Can you think about this for a moment?" I implore her. "Carmen, I just want you to be safe. You're my big sister. I want you to be happy for real. Not just put on a show for everyone. Years of faking it and silently suffering will destroy you. It will suck the life out of you, and you'll be dead inside."

"I will be fine," she assures me, putting a hand on my arm. "Don't worry about me. Besides, I can live vicariously through you—at least you have Liam! He seems like a great guy who would never..."

"Ha! I just met him yesterday."
"What?"
"He's a stranger," I admit shamefully.

Loretta Lost

"Sorry, Carm. He's just my doctor. I asked him to pretend for me."

"Oh." Her voice is empty and disappointed. "Well, then we're both fucked."

"Yeah," I agree.

"I guess... I'm going to go get married now," she says quietly. "Are you going to come stand beside me at the altar?"

"No." There is zero hesitation in my voice. "I don't support your decision. I can't be part of this celebration." My face contorts into a nasty frown. "But if Grayson dies, please invite me to his funeral."

"Okay," she says softly. "Thanks for coming to my wedding, Hellie. You're—you're the only one who *really* cares." Carmen throws her arms around me in one final, tight hug before leaving the library.

I could feel all her love and fear in the fierceness of her embrace. It brings tears to my eyes. I listen to her hurried footsteps as she turns and rushes across the foyer to do her duty and walk down the aisle. I know that she's just trying to be strong and do the right thing. Who am I to judge? Maybe it is the right thing to do. Maybe Grayson really is a good person with some sort of mental illness, and maybe the good he does in the world makes up for his sins. Maybe the good he does for my family makes up for what he did to me. Maybe he really will be a good father.

CLARITY 2

Somehow, I have trouble believing this.

The news of my sister's pregnancy is bittersweet. She seems excited at the prospect, and I will be happy to be an auntie. I wonder if Dad knows? Either way, I'm sure he would be thrilled. I just always imagined this happening under different circumstances. I imagined more laughter and safety. I imagined that it would be slow and carefully planned. I imagined throwing baby showers and parties, and celebrating with friends. I imagined that Mom would be there to help Carmen and guide her with good advice.

I imagined looking up to my big sister as she succeeded in life and accomplished huge milestones. I imagined patterning myself off her, and using her achievements to give me direction. I imagined her guiding me with her greater years and wisdom, and helping me feel certain on my own path. I imagined so much stupid bullshit that will never happen. Sure, I somewhat expected to use her mistakes to guide me on what *not* to do, but not to this extent.

This is not a mistake. This is a tragedy.

I slowly make my way out of the library, but I only get as far as the doorframe before I have to lean against the wall for support. It's my fault. If I had been braver, and tried to find my attacker instead of simply running away... I could have prevented this. I knew some information about him—although I'm not sure if it was accurate. I knew that he was an engineer and a football player. Those could have been lies, but I could have provided a general description of his physical build. I knew where he was, and at what time—there could have been security footage on the campus to show who was in the vicinity.

I was selfish and self-absorbed. I thought it was just about me, and my drama. I thought that if no one else had to hear my story and deal with the event, that they would all be safe. I thought that pretending it never happened could make it go away.

I thought it only happened to me because of my disability. I thought that by being blind, I was somehow asking for it. I thought that by crying in a stairwell, I had made myself vulnerable and an easy target; I announced myself as a victim, and it was almost entirely my fault. I thought that other women—normal women—would be able to look at a man and instantly see all the evil and cruelty inside him written on his face. Shouldn't those things be glaringly obvious?

It's my fault. It's all my fault. I could have protected her. I believed I was protecting her from the harshness of the truth, but really, I was concealing knowledge from her and exposing her to the harshness of reality. Now, she's pregnant. *He* made her pregnant. Probably without her consent or any planning. I failed her. I failed my sister.

CLARITY 2

She's not even thirty years old, but her life is over.

I hear the music quiet down and the minister begin to commence the ceremony. Each word is more grating to my ears than nails on a chalkboard. I can't stay in the house and listen to this anymore. I hate myself for what I've done. For letting this happen. How could I have been so stupid?

I hear footsteps on the hardwood floor of the foyer. Footsteps moving toward me.

"Helen?" says a worried male voice. "What's going on? Why aren't you in the ceremony?"

My mouth opens for me to speak, but I find that my lips are trembling. My eyebrows crease as I fight back tears of failure and self-hatred. "I shouldn't have come here, Liam." I take a moment to compose myself, trying to detach myself from the doorframe and stand up properly. My knee quivers slightly under me, threatening to cave. I did not walk around very much during the years that I spent confined to my little cabin, and I suppose I am kind of skinny and weak. My emotional state does not help. In this moment, I wish more than anything that I could be back home in my cabin. This place is not my home any longer.

"Is there anything I can do to help?" he asks me.

"No. Just..." I shut my eyes tightly to restrain my tears. "Please go away. Do your experiments on someone else. I don't want to be here. I don't want to be able to see."

"But Helen, we made a deal..."

"I don't even know why you bothered," I tell him. I am suddenly filled with rage, and I step forward to glare at the spot where I believe his face is. "Why do you even care? What the hell is your problem? Searching me out, and digging me out of my comfort zone. Dragging me back here, and trying to change everything about me? Trying to improve my life? What is your deal? Maybe you should mind your own business, Dr. Larson."

"Helen, this study really could change your life. Your vision is important. I don't know what upset you, but it has nothing to do with..."

"Fuck you!" I snap at him cruelly. "Vision is nothing. Vision is worthless. I am more than just a pair of broken eyes!"

"I never felt that way! I just wanted to help. I never meant to imply that..."

"No. I am not some pitiful disabled patient you can jerk around as you please, to suit your purposes. I *liked* my life in New Hampshire. I liked my shitty food, and I liked my shitty job, and I liked being alone. I *like* not being able to see, because I know there's a whole lot of ugly shit in the world. Isn't it bad enough that I have to *hear* it, and *feel* it? Did you ever think that being able to see it would cause my brain to explode in a sensory overload? You know I was on anti-depressants. Did you ever think it might be too

CLARITY 2

much, and I might end up in a mental institution for the rest of my life because I was forced to see things too clearly? See all these terrible things?"

"There are wonderful things too," Liam tells me. "Please, Helen. Just trust me. I wanted to show you so many beautiful things. Of course, it will be a huge adjustment when you first gain your vision, but it will make life so much easier in the long run. Trust me; it will be worth it. For every horrible thing you will see in the world, there will be a thousand amazing sights that far outshine the negative ones."

His voice is pleading and kind, and it cuts right down to my soul. I really do want to trust him and believe in the good things. I want to embrace the good that life has to offer, but how can I after this wedding? In the background of our conversation, wedding vows are being spoken as my sister signs away her soul to the devil.

"I, Carmen, take you, Grayson, to be my lawfully wedded husband from this day forward. In the presence of God, our family and friends..."

A tear that has been gathering in the corner of my eye finally breaks free. I feel helpless and overwhelmed. I feel even worse for being mean to Liam when I know that he has only been good to me in the short time we've been acquainted. I breathe deeply and exhale. "I'm sorry," I manage to say through a constricted throat. "This is the worst day I've had in years. Possibly the worst day

of my life. I just... I need to go."
"Helen, I..."
"No. Thank you for everything, Liam. Please excuse me." I turn and run through the house as quickly as I can. I need to get out of this place.

CLARITY 2

Chapter Four

I head toward the back of the house. My high-heeled shoes pound the ground as I run across the dining room, carefully stepping around chairs and other decorative pieces of furniture. I skirt around the kitchen counter as I head for the large glass doors that open out onto our patio. There is a small wooded area behind our house. It's not the perfect time of year to be going outside without a jacket, but I can't pause to properly prepare. I need to get out *now*. I am filled with rage, desperation, and guilt. I cannot seem to breathe, and I need fresh air.

Stepping through the door to the backyard, I slam it shut behind me. The cold air immediately pierces directly through my flimsy bridesmaid dress, and begins to stab at my skin like a blanket of tiny needles. Oddly enough, the first place it strikes me is my chest. I am not wearing bra, and my nipples begin to ache before any other part of my body. It feels like they have been dipped in liquid nitrogen, and scalded so badly that they

Loretta Lost

might fall off at any moment. I ignore this and continue to run across our backyard in my pumps, ignoring that the snow is seeping through the open toes of the shoes, and snapping around my ankles like bear traps made of ice. As I move down the patio steps and into the grass, the snow gets deeper, and begins to freeze my calves. Nevertheless, I move forward. I run through the snow until my skin is searing and blistering from the cold.

A couple times, I stumble, but I just manage to keep my balance and prevent myself from entirely falling. Finally, my heel catches on a dense snowdrift, and I do fall completely. My hands plunge forward into the snow to steady myself. It feels like icy fists have gripped my wrists as I struggle to pick myself off the ground. I realize that I'm not going to get anywhere in these shoes, and I reach down to rip them off my feet and angrily toss them across the backyard. Fuck this wedding, and fuck those shoes. Fuck this whole fucking day. I trudge through the snow barefoot, and get a kind of sick pleasure from the pain running up my legs, stabbing me like lightning bolts made of ice. I imagine getting serious frostbite and having to cut my feet off. It makes me move even faster.

Finally, knowing that I am nearing my destination, I begin to stretch my arms outward. I move around frantically, feeling for the impact of a

CLARITY 2

familiar structure. It takes a few minutes, and I begin to panic as I am lost and disoriented and standing knee-deep in bone-chilling snow. What if the structure I'm searching for has been moved or replaced in my absence? I sigh thankfully when my arms connect with the wooden walls of the garden shed. The cold surface feels sticky under my hands due to being coated with a thin layer of ice. Dragging my hands across the exterior of the shed, my fingers glide over the frosty glass windows. I slide my hands lower as I wildly search for the doorknob. It takes me a few seconds to locate the frigid metal knob, and I grasp it and turn violently, yanking the door open.

    Stepping into the old garden shed, I hastily close the door behind me. Only then do I exhale in relief. When I breathe in, my nostrils are filled with the scent of old wood and rusty metal gardening tools. There is also the lingering aroma of potted soil and dead plants. These decaying herbs used to be alive and flourishing when my mother tended the garden, and taken inside annually to be protected from the winter. Now, they are neglected and crumbling into dust. I begin moving through the garden shed to the other end, and my knee knocks over what must be a shovel. It clatters loudly to the ground, startling me. I always get really clumsy when I'm upset. I simply stop caring about the fact that I'm blind, and pretend that I'm invincible and magically know where everything is all around me. I boldly take another two steps, as though defying all inanimate objects and daring them to collide with me. On my third step, my heel jams down on the hard spikes of a rake. I curse and reflexively rip my foot away from the painful metal implement. My bare feet are already very sensitive and sore from the cold, so the agony caused by the impact is amplified at least tenfold. I clutch my sore foot with a wounded expression on my face as I glare down at my attacker.

There is a burst of fire in my gut as I reach forward and grasp the handle of the offensive rake. My arms move without my permission, swinging the rake madly and smashing it into the wall of the cabin, as though everything is its fault. I let out a scream as I slam the rake into the cabin's window, and the sound of shattering glass is heard. I let it fall down around me like lethal rain. It is extremely cathartic. For a moment, I feel strong and powerful. I feel like I could do anything.

Then it's gone. I am powerless. I remember everything.

I can't bear the crushing weight of these vile memories, and I need to escape them somehow. Running away to the ends of the earth won't help, and neither will smashing everything in sight. I need to disappear into my own mind.

Feeling guilty for my violent outburst, I try to carefully step around the stray shards of glass as I

CLARITY 2

move toward the corner of the little shed. I put my back toward the wall and slide down to the ground, and my bottom lands against the floor with a small thud. The cold ground sends icy shockwaves up through my dress, and I seriously regret wearing Carmen's thong. It is not offering much in the way of protection from the weather. This entire ensemble is worthless, and I might as well be naked. She even forced me to shave my legs! What I wouldn't give for even that extra protective layer of tiny hairs right now. Rubbing my hands up and down my clammy, cold legs, I try to get warm. I try to no avail. Blowing some hot air over my legs, I slap my toes to make sure I can feel them. They are so cold that it's excruciating. I press my hands against my chest, trying to soothe my stinging nipples. The coldness is no longer jabbing me with needles, but with dagger-like intensity.

However, I am glad for the pain. It distracts me from the memories that are playing across the inside of my mind—the memories that I can't seem to shake away. So many parts of my body are screaming at me for attention that I don't even know where to begin. I reach forward I wrap my fingers around my frozen toes to try to massage the sensation back into them, but before long, my hands start feeling too cold to assist my toes. I stick my fingers under my armpits to help them defrost, but I am soon distracted by the throbbing ache in my ears. I lift my hands to cup my tender ears for a moment. As I close my eyes, I hear Grayson's voice echoing in my mind. I am frustrated to find that even though I have left the house, and even though I have my hands clamped over my ears, the man is too deep inside my head for me to find sanctuary. It's completely futile to fight against both the cold and the past.

The strength and fire within me quickly dissipate. I slump weakly against the side of the wall. I stop caring about my painful ears and toes, and just wrap my arms around my legs. I hug my knees tightly against my chest and curl up into a little ball. I rock slightly back and forth in an attempt to soothe and warm myself. I can't think. I want to comfort myself with reassuring thoughts about my own strength and resilience, but I just can't think.

I sit there by myself for several minutes, enjoying the solitude.

My mind floats away, and I am at peace again.

I remain in this state until a loud noise causes me to jump in fright. I realize that someone is opening the door of the garden shed. I gasp and freeze in panic, as my heart rate instantly doubles. Is the wedding over? Is it Grayson? Has he come looking for me? I want to move forward to grab the metal rake for protection, or maybe a sliver of broken glass from the window I smashed, but I can't seem to make my body move. Is it him? Is he

CLARITY 2

here to torture me again?

I hear the man's breathing, and my cold fingers are suddenly reenergized. I reach forward, fumbling for the rake. I grasp the handle firmly, ready to swing it again—this time, directly into that bastard's skull.

"What is it with you and little wooden shacks?" says Liam's teasing voice. "I bet you were the kind of kid who played with a cardboard box even when you were given really expensive, fancy toys."

I open my fingers and let the rake clatter to the ground. I am so thankful to hear Liam's voice. I am so relieved that it's him. I feel a rush of emotion pouring through the floodgates. I can't restrain this onslaught of gladness mixed in with anguish. It shakes me to my very core. I place my face in my hands.

"Helen?" he says softly. "My god, you're shaking like a leaf. What happened?"

A few tears tumble into my hands, and my shoulders shudder slightly. I take a deep breath, and find my resolve. "I'm just cold," I say in a small and halting voice. It is the best explanation I could muster, and quite obviously a blatant lie.

"Of course you're cold!" he says angrily. "You're running through the snow half-naked like a madwoman. Do you want to get hypothermia? Jesus, Helen! I said I could fix your eyes. I can't get you a new pair of legs, too."

Loretta Lost

In spite of myself, a smile tugs at my lips. My moment of mirth is interrupted by a violent shiver, and I hug my knees closer to my chest. I have never felt such severe, almost unbearable pain in my nipples before. I did not know how much they could hurt. "Why didn't you just go home?" I ask him.

"I thought about it," he says, entering the cabin and closing the door behind him. "I got in my car and turned on the engine. But then I looked down and saw that paperback you signed for me. With that personalized inscription. 'Please leave me alone.' I suppose it's the rebel in me, but I simply couldn't let you have the satisfaction."

"Thanks," I tell him quietly. "Sorry I was such a bitch earlier. I'm actually... glad you're here."

Liam moves over to my corner of the shed, stepping over the shovels and rakes. When he's standing directly above me, I hear the rustling of fabric as he removes his coat. In the next moment, he is laying the thick garment over my bare legs and arms.

I stare down at the coat in surprise. Of course, I see nothing, but the kindness in his gesture has caused me to feel as though he has placed a glowing cloak of magical diamonds at my feet. I am overwhelmed with emotion; I value this so much. I know that it's a tiny, basic thing that any person should do, but not every person *does*.

CLARITY 2

Grayson wouldn't. When faced with someone sad and down on her luck, he wouldn't help. He would take advantage of the situation. I am so thankful that Liam is not like him.

The truth is that I am already so frozen that his coat does very little for my temperature. Still, I treasure the thoughtfulness of the act. I probably needed a bit of sensitivity and caring far more than I needed to be warm. I carefully extend my fingers to touch Liam's coat. It's difficult to move my hands, because my fingers are so stiff. I run my fingers over the lining of the fabric, just to convince myself that this is real—the coat is a symbol that there is at least one good person in the world. I can barely feel the coarse fibers under what is surely the beginning of frostbitten digits, but it is reassuring to know that they are there. Liam's compassion causes a tiny spark that begins to thaw the cold and dead parts of me that matter far more than my skin.

"It's dangerous to be out here like this," he tells me, crouching down to my level. "Jesus, Helen. Your lips are turning blue. We should go back inside."

"I'm not going back into that house," I say adamantly. "I'd rather die here."

"But Helen..."

"No. I told you I had a bad feeling. I never should have come back here."

Liam takes my hands into his and begins to

rub them between his own to generate some heat through friction. "You're shivering way too much. Let me go inside and get some warmer clothes and some blankets..."

"No, I'm fine." I pull my hands away from him and wrap them around myself.

I hear him standing up and moving briskly toward the exit of the shed. "I should grab some hot cocoa at the very least, and maybe a portable heater..."

"No—no. Liam. Please don't leave. Just stay with me?" I can't believe how pathetic I sound. I can't believe that sentence even left my lips. My embarrassment is quickly assuaged when I feel the floorboards creak as he moves back over to my corner, and lowers himself to sit next to me. I am relieved to have him near me, but I am swiftly seized with a fear that he will get *too* close. I remember Grayson's hands on my body, and the gun against my chest. I remember the disgusting, degrading kiss. I flinch away from Liam, pressing myself against the wall of the wooden cabin. I feel a sudden suffocating claustrophobia. I am not usually one to dislike small spaces—in fact, I usually prefer them—but being confined in close quarters with other people is entirely unnerving.

I am grateful when Liam maintains his distance. He does not try to embrace me or move any closer; not even under the pretense of keeping me warm. He seems to be able to sense my

CLARITY 2

anxiety. When he sits beside for over a full minute without trying to touch me or even asking why I'm upset, I begin to relax. I stop holding my breath, and I feel the erratic pounding of my heart slowly ease. I reach down and lift his coat, arranging it so that it covers his legs as well.

"Can I at least keep trying to warm your hands?" he asks me. "I'm worried."

"Yes," I tell him softly, "but I think my toes are the real problem. They feel like they're going to fall off."

I feel Liam slide his coat over my ankles to study my feet. "Helen... okay. This is going to sound awful, but you need to listen to me." He speaks in a brisk and commanding tone that I haven't heard him use before. "Put your feet in my lap."

"In your lap?" I say awkwardly.

"Yes. Unless you want to risk losing your toes."

"You're probably exaggerating," I accuse him, but the cold is so agonizing that I am beginning to grow desperate for any warmth. I try to flex my toes, and wince, because even that tiny bit of motion hurts like a bitch.

"I'm not really exaggerating. It's damn cold out here. But I won't let you get severe frostbite," he tells me firmly, "because I'll drag you kicking and screaming back into that house before any permanent damage is done. However, if you don't follow my instructions right away, you'll probably develop blisters and swelling so painful that you can't walk for days."

I make a face, for this sounds almost as unpleasant as my feet already feel.

"Trust me," he says. "I'm a doctor."

"You know that every time you say that I get even more suspicious, right?" I ask him lightly.

"Feet. Lap. Now." He demands this while vigorously rubbing my fingers.

Biting my lip, I angle my body perpendicular to his and place my feet in his lap. I carefully rest my toes against what should be the warmest part of his upper thigh, while still being as respectful and polite as possible and not plunging my toes directly into his genitals. Unfortunately, I am so numb that I can't feel any of his body heat and it offers no immediate relief to my stinging pain.

Liam arranges his coat more closely around my legs as he continues to rub my fingers.

"Thanks," I tell him softly.

"You don't need to thank me," he responds, and there is a bit of anger in his voice. "I'm just trying to keep you all in one piece. Jesus. It's like you're determined to sabotage yourself! If being blind isn't bad enough, you have no appreciation for your fingers and toes. Your body parts aren't just expendable, you know!"

"No," I tell him. "That's not what I meant. Thanks for not asking what happened in the

CLARITY 2

house."

"Oh," he says in surprise. "Well... you're welcome. I figure that if you want to tell me, you will."

I am quiet for a moment, except for the noise of my teeth chattering and my short, rapid breathing. "Can I sit a little closer to you?" I ask quietly.

"Sure," he says, but he moves toward me instead, pinning me into the corner of the shed. He slips his arm around me, trying to cradle me in a cocoon of comfort and warmth.

I lean forward and press my shoulder against his body, trying to burrow into the warmth of his armpit. My ears and nose have been stinging with pain, and I press my face against his chest to steal the heat of his torso, through his tuxedo jacket. My feet are still positioned in his lap. I am shivering quite uncontrollably now, and running out into the snow no longer seems like it was the perfect rebellious and dramatic idea. It feels like it was immature and self-destructive. I wouldn't have cared if Liam hadn't followed me; if it was just me alone, shivering and getting frostbite and possibly dying, I might be comfortable with that. But forcing him to take care of me? Making him deal with my stress and my crisis? That's selfish of me, and it's not right. I feel so childish and needy, and I hate myself for being like this.

"I'm sorry," I mumble against his chest. "I

didn't mean to involve you..."

"I involved myself," he responds. "Are you feeling a bit warmer? Does it hurt anywhere?"

"Just my ears and face," I say quietly. My nipples are also hurting a great deal, but I am far too embarrassed to mention that. The cold is starting to make me sleepy.

I feel one of Liam's hands leave mine, and a warm palm is pressed against my exposed ear. He gently rubs my ear between his fingers, and I wince at the pain. I feel his fingers under my chin, lifting it so that he can examine my face. He presses his thumb against my nose, massaging it gently, followed by my cheeks. He leans down and breathes hot air into my face, and it tickles my eyelashes. He skirts his thumb over my frozen lips, while breathing more hot air onto my skin.

"Um," he says awkwardly, suddenly pulling away. "Sorry about that."

"About what?" I ask in confusion.

"You know..." He clears his throat. "The situation in my lap."

"Oh!" I say in surprise. I'm not sure why, but I try to wiggle my toes around to figure out what he's talking about. I am almost disappointed when all I feel is the burning pain of my toes. "Unfortunately, I'm too numb to feel anything and I hadn't noticed."

"Dammit. Then I shouldn't have mentioned it," he grumbles. "How humiliating. Can you

CLARITY 2

please stop poking your feet around now? That's not helping."

"Is something happening in your lap?" I ask innocently. For some reason, this is somewhat amusing to me. The gentle beginnings of a smile cause the corners of my lips to crinkle, and this hurts my face as though my skin is made of ice which has begun to crack and shatter.

"Helen," he says with warning. "Stop teasing me. You refused to go inside or let me go in the house and bring something warm back—so I'm improvising. This is the best I can do."

"Thanks," I tell him sincerely. I lean forward and press my face against his chest again, but this time it's not entirely for warmth. "Why was there a situation in your lap?" I ask him.

"Oh. I was just thinking of ways to help you get warm... and for an instant, the thought of kissing you might have crossed my mind."

Luckily, my face being hidden against his chest conceals my surprise. "Thanks for not doing that. I don't think I could handle it right now."

"You don't have to keep thanking me for being a decent human being, Helen. Besides, logically, my armpit is warmer, so you should probably stick your face there—it was just a fleeting thought I couldn't control."

I try to conceal a frown. I told him on the car ride over here that I had changed my name, and no longer wanted to be called Helen. My recent encounter with Grayson has only made it worse. I hate that name. I hate the way he says it. I hate everything associated with it. I wish that I could escape it, but I already tried that once. Someone still found me and brought me home. How could I escape even further? How could I really get away and disappear from all this?

My thoughts take a sinister turn, and I start wishing that Liam had not found me. I start to grow comforted by imagining a perfect silence and darkness, one even more complete than my usual silence and darkness. I think that Liam senses my train of thought, for he rubs his hand up and down over my back.

"What are you thinking about?" he asks softly.

I can't respond. How can I tell him these thoughts? How can I tell him that I am wishing I would freeze to death? He will think I'm insane. Still, I can't stop wishing that my existence would come to an end, so that I would never have to be afraid, anxious, or alone again. The last of those three qualities, the loneliness, is not something that I have allowed to bother me in the past. But after feeling a brief period of hopefulness and happiness, brought to me by Liam and his dorky friend Owen, I'm not sure how I can return to my previous life. After imagining for hours how glorious it could be to have my vision returned, and after hugging my dad again for the first time in

CLARITY 2

years, and eating scrumptious cupcakes—how can I give up all of this? Worst of all, is this precious feeling I currently have.

I feel like Liam has dropped everything to take care of me—not just to prevent my potential frostbite, but to comfort me emotionally. He hasn't mentioned it, but it is quite obvious in the careful way that he is holding me that he's not just here because I'm a patient. There was no need to follow me out into the backyard to check on me. Coming to the wedding *at all* was unnecessary, especially after I told him not to. Heck—it was crazy that he sought me out specifically for his experiment when there were probably dozens of other excellent candidates. Why would he go out of his way to be so nice? Everything he's done for me has been over-the-top and extraordinary. I haven't had to ask repeatedly for assistance, or pressure him, and grow to feel uncomfortable and desperate. He has just taken action, so easily and happily, almost completely without prompting. We did make a few silly bargains, but I think that was mostly having fun. He has helped me and been there for me, almost as though he might *enjoy* doing things for me.

And he's here right now. Suffering through the cold with me. Protecting me. From the weather, from Grayson, and from myself.

For the first time in as long as I can remember, I feel important to someone.

Loretta Lost

I feel like the center of his world.

It's ridiculous, I know—and I won't be foolish enough to say anything of the sort. It's just that since my mom died, I haven't felt this kind of sympathy and understanding. I haven't had any intimate connections with any other people—I haven't had anyone in whom I could confide. I've only known Liam for a few hours, but he really does feel like an old friend. It's so easy to talk to him, like we might have always been around each other, moving in the same circles, reading the same books, sharing the same experiences. I know this is insane and untrue, but there's just something calming about his energy. There's something true and solid in his voice.

Gone is the boisterous, animated sound of Carmen's shrill tone—she somehow managed to be peppy and animated even in her darkest moment. I don't think anything could keep that girl down. Thinking about her makes me feel a little sick. Our previous conversation really got under my skin. Sometimes listening to her speak can be exhausting, but that had to be the most depressing conversation we ever shared. In contrast, when Liam speaks, in his slow and careful way, I just want to hear more.

It baffles me that even though he has no idea what's wrong with me, or the reason why I ran out into the snow, he's helping anyway. No questions asked. I am suddenly overcome with the urge to

CLARITY 2

tell him. I am not sure why—do I require validation for my reckless act? Do I feel I owe him an explanation in exchange for his kindness? Or is the memory of Carmen and her situation destroying my insides like a cancer, and do I need to share it with someone in order to get it out of my system?

"Do you want to know what's bothering me?" I ask him, taking a frosty breath.

"I'm dying to know," he admits, "but only if you want to share."

Nodding, I try to find the words. "Remember the story I told you in the car? About my past? What happened to me?"

"Yes, of course," he answers.

I shut my eyes tightly. It feels like that car ride was a lifetime ago. So much has happened since then that I feel like a different person. I clear my throat as I prepare to deliver the awkward words. "The man that my sister just married... is the man who... yeah."

Liam sits up a little, and I feel his entire body tense up in understanding. He does not respond right away. He seems dumbstruck to the point of speechlessness. I can also feel that he has not taken a breath in several seconds as he processes the information. "You're saying that the groom—Grayson—is the one who..."

"Yeah."

He remains wordless for another little while.

Loretta Lost

"Does your sister know?"

"Not exactly. I mean—not about me. I tried to tell her, but I think she doesn't want to know." I hesitate and frown, rubbing my hands together for warmth. "He's exhibited the same sort of behavior with her."

"Then why the hell did you let them get married?" Liam shoves my legs off his lap and rises to his feet. "We have to call the police!"

"Liam, Liam... she's pregnant." I lower my face in disappointment at the situation. "She accepts him. She forgives him. Or at least that's what she tells herself," I mutter under my breath.

"I don't understand. How can—how can she...?" Liam pauses. "Is this a joke, Helen? I know you're a writer, so..."

I sigh and shiver at the freezing floorboards which are beneath my toes once again. "I wish it was a joke."

"This is possibly the most insane thing I've ever heard," Liam tells me.

I bitterly shrug my cold, bare shoulders. "Personally, I prefer fiction. This is what happens when I try to participate in real life."

Liam makes a derisive noise. "Fuck that guy. Don't let one assface ruin real life for you." The floorboards creak and the glass crunches as Liam paces back and forth in the garden shed. "I just don't understand how this happened. Was it a coincidence? Or did he do it on purpose?"

CLARITY 2

"I don't know," I say quietly. "I think it was on purpose—maybe because he felt guilty and wanted to help my family as repentance. Or maybe because he liked hurting me so much that he wanted the opportunity to emotionally torture me for the rest of my life. In addition to the other stuff."

"Jesus," Liam says harshly. "Jesus! Fuck."

"Yeah," I say again dryly, rubbing my arms.

"And your sister didn't care? She was cool with the whole thing?" Liam demands.

"She said she loves him," I respond. "She says that she considers it a mental illness and that she's going to counseling with him."

"Dammit!" Liam says, his voice escalating in volume. "What is wrong with these stupid women! Why do they always subject themselves to such bullshit? Do you know how many female patients I've seen not because of some random accident, infection, or congenital disease—but because of domestic abuse? And then they come back again. And again. And they beg me not to do anything about it. It's fucking bullshit!"

I am a little startled by his outburst. I didn't expect him to be so passionate about this subject. He is also defending me—he is on my side, and I feel like I have an ally.

The floorboards creak again as Liam paces furiously in the tiny garden shed. "It's a bit more understandable when they're from other cultures," he says heatedly. "I figure they have certain traditions, and that's just the way they've been raised to behave. It's hard to break ancient habits. But your sister is American. What the fuck is wrong with her?"

His righteous anger thrills me a little, and I do feel validated. "Thank you."

"Dammit," Liam says again. "I'm really upset. I don't even *know* Carmen, but I'm so pissed at her. I kind of want to grab this shovel or rake and just smash it into the wall a few times."

A sardonic smile comes to my lips. "Be my guest. Try taking out the other window. Smashing this one really helped me feel better."

"Oh, you did that?" Liam pauses. "What are we going to do? We need to do something about this, right? Should we call the cops anyway?"

"I don't know. That could make things worse." I suddenly find that my lip is quivering and I'm getting emotional. I was trying to remain aloof and above this, and not let Liam see how much it's affecting me, but it's getting increasingly difficult the more we discuss this. "He has a gun—he threatened me," I say quietly. I lift my hands to massage my temples gently, and take a deep breath. "When I spoke to him... he seemed to genuinely want to be with Carmen. He said he would shoot her and then himself if I did anything to stop the wedding. He put the gun against my chest so I could feel it."

CLARITY 2

"Oh, Helen," Liam says. "I'm so sorry..."

"Don't call me that," I whisper. I slightly shift my hands so that they cover my ears. "Why does everyone call me that? I'm not her anymore."

I feel the floor shift beneath me as Liam comes closer. He kneels before me and places a hand on my shoulder.

"Winter," he says softly, as if testing it on his tongue. "Winter, please listen to me. You're right. You're not the same person, and that man is not going to hurt you ever again. Do you believe me?"

His words filter through my hands, and I cautiously remove them from my ears. I swallow, trying to fight back tears. "But he's going to hurt *her*. He literally has a *license* to hurt her. He's going to hurt my unborn niece or nephew. And it's all my fault."

"Don't say that," he tells me firmly. "This is definitely not your fault. Not in any way."

"But it is," I say brokenly. "I ran away from home. I kept everything to myself. If I had stayed here, I could have prevented this. I could have protected her. I would have recognized him sooner—I could have warned her early on, before she was so attached to him and *pregnant*. Now it's too late."

Liam hesitates. "What if... what if the gun thing was just bravado? What if he really has changed?"

Loretta Lost

"You're just saying that," I accuse him. "You're just trying to make me feel better."

"Not entirely. I'm being serious. Do you believe in redemption?"

I blink a few times as I consider this. The intensity of the conversation and our emotions have almost entirely distracted me from the cold, and I shiver a little. "Redemption? I don't know. Have you ever known someone who really changed?"

"Not really," he responds. "I just—I guess I just think it's a nice idea." Liam comes to sit by my side again, and he takes my feet back into his lap. He begins to rub my toes to stimulate circulation and keep them warm.

We sit like this, in silence for several minutes. My thoughts turn to the future, and what my plan of action should be. I feel so weak and miserable, and incapable of dealing with this.

"So this is why you don't want to participate in the study anymore?" he asks me.

"What?" I say in confusion, startled from my thoughts.

"Earlier when you were yelling at me, you said you didn't want me to try the gene therapy on your eyes. Were you just upset, or did you mean that?"

I shake my head, with my eyebrows drawn together in a frown. It's difficult to speak. "I wish I could do the study. I wish it more than anything.

CLARITY 2

But now? I can't stay here in this house. In this city. I have to get the hell away from this place."

"But don't you regret running away last time?" he asks me.

"Yes, but..." I try to think of how to phrase my thoughts. "I already failed. What more damage could really be done? Even if I do stay—I'm powerless to protect Carmen or make things better. I might even make things worse with my presence."

"You have to stay," Liam insists. "You can't just leave again. You have this huge opportunity, and if you run away... then he's won. You can't let him destroy your life."

"Luckily, I hardly have any life for him to destroy. Not here. I don't have any ties to this place. My life is sitting in a small cabin up north, and that's where I should return. I haven't called to cancel my grocery deliveries yet. I should just go back there."

"I won't let you," Liam tells me. "The life you were living was no kind of life at all. It was some kind of masochistic self-punishment for something that wasn't even your fault. You need to stay here and be strong, Hel—Winter. Stay here, and let me try to give you the ability to see."

"I don't think I can..."

"You can't let a ghost from your past destroy your future."

"It doesn't feel like he's in the past anymore,

Liam. He's right here. He's standing a few steps away in my family home... he's probably laughing and feeding my sister cake right now."

Liam makes a sound of exasperation. "Well, fuck him! You can't go on running and hiding from everything good just because of this one man. What about me? I mean, ignoring the fact that you *promised* that if we drove you home, you'd let us do the research..."

"I'm sorry to go back on my word," I say glumly. "I didn't expect that it would be unsafe to be here."

"*Ignoring* that fact," Liam repeats with emphasis, "what about us?"

"Us?" I repeat slowly.

"Yeah. Am I crazy," he asks, "or is there something here between us?"

My lips part to deliver a response, but I press them together again tightly to save myself from saying something impulsive and possibly stupid.

"Maybe it's just friendship," Liam says. "Maybe... there's the potential for something more. I don't know, but I just... I really like being around you." He clears his throat awkwardly. "Am I nuts? Do you feel the same?"

I close my eyes before speaking, almost ashamed of the answer. "Yes," I say weakly.

"Good," he says, exhaling in relief. "It's just special, you know? It's rare to meet someone and have such an awesome connection right off the bat.

CLARITY 2

You can't just toss *us* away before we even know what *us* could be." His voice grows firm and demanding. "I'm sorry if saying this is uncool, or if it makes you uncomfortable. I just won't accept you *banishing* yourself from the realm to live in exile again. This house is your kingdom, and you can't let some fool shove you out of your domain."

I can't help but smile sadly in spite of myself at the adorable metaphor.

"If this is a territorial dispute, you need to mark your space and hold your ground," Liam says with determination. "He doesn't deserve to take everything that's yours. He doesn't deserve to win. He doesn't deserve to steal your family, and steal all possibility of you having friends or lovers..."

I lower my face to conceal a blush at that last word. Somehow, even though I am literally freezing my ass off (it is now conclusive that I despise thongs with a great passion) my cheeks begin to feel very hot at the concept of having a lover. My feet are still in Liam's lap, and my mind drifts back to his earlier apology about his body's responsiveness to me. The thought that someone kind and intelligent might actually desire *me* is quite wonderful. It gives me a little injection of self-esteem and strength. But then I remind myself that it's so wonderful it's almost *unbelievable*. Something about the whole situation seems too good to be true.

"I just want to see you again," Liam says.

Loretta Lost

"That can't happen if you go away. I want to be your friend. I want to read your new book before everyone else. I want you to be happy. I want to be there on the day that you get your vision back, and see the look on your face."

"Liam," I say softly. "That's all a lovely fantasy, but..."

"It's not a fantasy," he assures me. "All of this can happen if you just stay here and *trust me*."

I take a moment to consider his words before responding. A deep frown settles into my face. I try to breathe slowly and evenly to clear my mind as I carefully choose my next words. "Do you want to know what I'm afraid of, Liam?"

"What is it?" he asks, squeezing my knee.

I take another deep breath before responding. Tears prick the back of my eyes, and I fend them off with a halfhearted smile. "What scares me most is that even if I *could* see, I would still be blind to the truth about people. Like Carmen." I wrinkle my eyes, struggling to repress the waterworks. "She can't tell what a demon he is—and I'm supposed to be the blind one. What if being able to see actually distracts a person from the truth of things, beneath the surface? What if I saw a pretty face and thought there must be an equally beautiful soul behind it? I'm sitting here with you, and I have no clue what you look like, except for other people's descriptions. But I can hear your voice, and your words, and feel your touch—and I think

CLARITY 2

you're wonderful. But I could still be wrong. This could all be deception. I have been wrong before. What if I could see you, and you were beautiful? What if I were enchanted by your outward appearance? How would I have *any* indication that there could be a monster deep inside you? How could I possibly protect myself? What if having perfect eyesight actually made things worse for me—what if being able to see more made me understand less? What if the world became less clear?" I pause, realizing that I have been going on and on in an emotional tirade. I lift my fingertips and press them against my closed eyelid as a tear squeezes itself through the crevice. I sigh and utter one final sentence to Liam in closing:

"You can give me vision, but you can't give me clarity."

Liam reaches out and presses his palm against my cheek. He stares at me silently for a brief interval before speaking. "Winter," he says softly. "The name does suit you. You're as pure as the snow. Your mind is like the crisp, clean winter air."

I puzzled by his romantic response.

"I will give you clarity, Winter," he promises in a low voice. "I'll give you everything I possibly can."

The tone of devotion in his oath is so strong that I can't bear it. I press my hands against my face as the tears begin to fall freely. I want to

Loretta Lost

believe him so badly. I want to believe that things will be fine. "I was so happy, Liam. Earlier on, with you and Owen. I was the happiest I've been in ages. Everything seemed good."

"I know," he says, hugging me gently. "When I texted Owen, I told him to try his best to make you laugh."

Once again, I am stunned by Liam's thoughtfulness. That he would care at all about making a stranger laugh is unreal. It causes more tears to slide down my cheeks. "What am I going to do?" I ask him. "How can I live in the same house with that man? He threatened to kill my sister and her baby."

"Just take it one step at a time," he tells me. "One day at a time. You might find that once you rid yourself of fear, life will surprise you and you'll learn a great deal."

His words of wisdom are somehow soothing; even when I'm in this state. For an instant, I recognize how vulnerable I am. Liam is already incredibly nice, but compared to Grayson, he seems like a storybook hero. I am not in a good place to be making decisions or judgments about anything or anyone. I really don't have any clarity. Maybe I never did.

"I would like to invite you out on a date," Liam suddenly says.

"A date?" I ask guardedly.

"Yes. I spoke to Dr. Howard earlier, and I

CLARITY 2

told her about your granola-bar-and-protein-shake diet..."

"Don't forget the wine. I also drank wine," I inform him stubbornly.

"That doesn't help too much with your overall nutrition," he says lightly. "Leslie is concerned about your health and wants to run a full physical on you and some diagnostic tests on Thursday, before we proceed with the clinical study. At this rate, she might also have to treat you for frostbite."

"That doesn't sound much like a date to me."

"Oh, not that!" He laughs lightly. "I meant that maybe I could pick you up and take you to the appointment, and we could hang out afterwards."

"I would like to—but isn't that unethical?" I ask him.

"Yes," he says softly. "It would technically be unethical for me to date you until after the study is complete, and some time has passed. Otherwise, it puts my career in jeopardy."

"Oh," I say in disappointment. "Well, we shouldn't risk it. I understand."

He seems to ponder over this briefly. "Or maybe... I could *not* be ethical," he suggests.

"Yes," I tell him quietly. "Please. Please—don't be ethical. I don't need ethical right now."

He takes my hand and puts reassuring pressure on my palm. "Then I'll see you on

Thursday," he says decisively. "I'll plan something awesome for us to do, to take your mind off all of this."

"I doubt you can take my mind off this," I say skeptically.

"I'll consider that a challenge," he says with a chuckle. "But for now, let's get you inside and get you warm. For god's sake, woman. What will your father think of me? It's not a good first impression that I let his daughter get turned into a popsicle."

The mention of popsicles makes me smile in memory of Owen's stories. After sitting and chatting with Liam, I am definitely feeling better and stronger. When I let him guide me to my feet, I am not so terrified of the future. It helps to have one pleasant thing to look forward to.

CLARITY 2

Chapter Five

I toss and turn between the sheets.

I have been locked in my bedroom for days. I have no idea how I'm going to last until Thursday.

After the wedding I had the housekeeper help me move my suitcase from my old bedroom to one of the guest rooms on the other side of the house. It is closer to my dad's bedroom, and as far as possible from Carmen and Grayson's new room. Of course, it also has its own bathroom, and *not* one that opens into any other rooms. Choosing this strategic location has made me feel slightly more at ease. I even asked the housekeeper to study the outside of the house and make sure that the window wasn't easily accessible by climbing up any drainpipes. She probably thought I was crazy. I figured that I could keep to the safety of this room for the most part, but venture out into the rest of the house when Grayson was at work. But it just so happens that he was able to get many vacation days to celebrate his wedding.

Unfortunately, he didn't use them to go on

Loretta Lost

vacation.

    I'm not sure why they didn't go on a honeymoon—I think it's because Grayson wanted to keep an eye on me. Either way, I have been unable to leave the room. That in itself is not so terrible. I am used to being confined to a small space and not moving around much. However, I have been entirely unable to work. Every time I tried, I found myself sitting uselessly before my braille typewriter, with my hands resting lightly on the keys. Try as I might, I could not seem to make my fingers move to produce anything worthwhile. All I could think about was that *he* was right outside my door.

    Sometimes my father tried to coax me out to join the family for dinner, but I tried to decline as politely as possible, making excuses about how I needed privacy for my writing. In the middle of the night, I was able to scavenge for a large case of bottled water, in addition to a six-pack of soda. I also secured a few jars of peanut butter, some raisins, bags of chips, and cheese. These items are my only sustenance, and they must last until Grayson leaves the house again, and I can finally get more food. I locked the bedroom door and used several pieces of furniture to barricade myself inside. Pushing the dresser was difficult, but once I temporarily removed the drawers, it became easier.

    Now, I have no idea what day it is. Possibly Tuesday or Wednesday. I am also unsure whether

CLARITY 2

it is night or day. Liam has called me a few times to make small talk, but he has been busy at work and hasn't had much time to spare. For the most part, I have been trying to sleep to pass the time. (It also requires the least expenditure of energy and helps my food last longer since I don't need to consume quite as much.) I have been rolling around in bed for hours, trying to think of my story and imagine the scenes I intend to write later on, so there is at least some meager attempt at working. Mostly, I just let my mind run away with me and dream, and do as it wishes to do. This could be therapeutic in clearing the blockage in my brain and allowing my imagination to flow freely again.

I am focused on the bright colors and stories of my dreamscape when a knock sounds on the door. I try to coax myself into being awake as I pull myself off the bed.

"Dad?" I ask in confusion. "I can't come out to eat today. Not until I finish this book."

"It's not your father," Grayson responds.

In an instant, I am extremely awake. My hands tightly grip and twist bunches of the comforter.

"Your dad told me to bring some of your favorite cupcakes for you," Grayson says gently. "Why don't you come downstairs and spend some time with us? We can catch up."

I can't believe his gall in acting like nothing

Loretta Lost

is wrong. In acting like we could be a happy family and eat cupcakes together. "No, thank you," I say through the door. "I'm not hungry." My stomach immediately growls at this lie.

"You don't have to come downstairs if you don't feel like it," Grayson tells me. He pauses. "I could just hand you the cupcakes and leave."

"No, thank you," I say again. My mind begins to race, and I begin to grow worried. "Where is my sister?" I demand.

"She went out to a doctor's appointment for the pregnancy," Grayson tells me. "She's fine—it's just a routine checkup."

"Why didn't you go with her?" I ask him.

"I told her I had some things to take care of here."

My eyebrows furrow deeply. "Then go take care of them," I tell him.

"I am," he says.

I sit up straighter in alarm when the doorknob starts rattling as he tries to gain entry to my room. Swinging my legs out of bed, I walk over to the dresser that blocks my door from opening, and I abruptly sit down with my back against the furniture. I figure that even if he is able to somehow unlock my door, maybe I can use my body to push against the dresser and keep it from opening.

"Come on. Let me in, Helen," he demands. "I just want to talk."

CLARITY 2

"Go away," I tell him.

"Really, your dad's getting worried about you. I think it would ease his mind if you came out of your room and ate a few of these cupcakes."

It occurs to me that my dad probably took Carmen to her doctor's appointment. That means I'm alone in the house with Grayson. My cell phone is over on my night table, but I decide to bluff anyway.

"If you don't get the hell away from my door and stop bothering me right now, I will call the cops," I tell him quietly.

"Don't be like that," Grayson tells me. He sighs, and I hear him put his back to the door and slide to sit down just outside the bedroom. "I just want to talk about what happened between us. I mean, don't you wants answers? Aren't you curious?"

"No."

"I'm your brother-in-law now, Helen. You should be nicer to me. We should be friends."

"Fuck you," I hiss. Anger and fear are bubbling up inside me like a storm. I don't think I can take living in this house anymore. Not even for Liam—not even for the prospect of getting my vision back. This is not living. I have no freedom and I am completely unable to work. Liam said that staying was the stronger thing to do, but I don't feel like I can keep fighting against my fear on a daily basis. It wins. Each and every time, it

Loretta Lost

wins.

"I know what I did to you was wrong," he says, "but I just couldn't help myself. That day, when you were sitting and crying on the stairs in the engineering department, it wasn't the first time I had ever seen you."

I sink my teeth into my bottom lip to try to keep from responding and betraying how upsetting this is.

"I'd been watching you for weeks," Grayson admits softly. "I thought you were really cute, and I wanted to ask you out... but I didn't know how to do that. I used to be really shy when it came to women. So, I followed you. I memorized your schedule, and I would watch you enter your classes, and wait until they were over, and watch you head back to your dorm."

I was being stalked. The realization that I had no idea that this was happening hits me like a ton of bricks. All this time, I thought it was just a random attack. If I could see—if I had been able to see, I might have noticed that I was being followed. I press the palms of my hands into my eyes, hating my body for being so flawed. I inwardly curse my disability.

"There was just something special about you, Helen. There always was. I watched you moving through the crowds of people with this serene look on your face. You just seemed like someone holy to me. Someone greater than everyone else. I spent

CLARITY 2

weeks following you, and studying you from afar, and trying to gather the courage to talk to you."

I take a shuddering breath. Listening to this story is filling me with horror. I don't want to hear his perspective. I don't want to revisit this event. I just want it to be finished and over.

"Your hair was the color of mahogany, but when you stepped into the sunlight, it burst into flames like the strands were made of copper. I couldn't stop staring at your tawny locks, and the way they curled around your perfect face. I was just so drawn to you, Helen. I've never felt that way about anyone. It was like you were calling out to me. Like touching you was part of my destiny."

"Please stop," I say in a hoarse voice. "Please stop talking about this. Please go away."

"Then a day came when something changed. I could see the change in your face. Your eyes, they used to shine like burnished amber. But on this day, they were just dead. They were empty, like sand or rust. You didn't go to class. You wandered aimlessly until you just collapsed and crumbled into tears. You were sad. I've never seen you so sad, Helen."

I can't listen to this. His retelling makes everything fresh. I can feel the way I felt that day, even before he made my day worse. I shake my head, unable to believe that this is happening to me.

"That was the first day I could find the

courage to talk to you," Grayson said. "I had to say something. I had to try to lift you up and be your hero."

I swallow a bit of saliva that has been gathering in my throat. "When I first heard you speak," I manage to croak out, "I thought you were nice. You could have asked me out. I would have probably agreed."

"I wanted to," he admits. "More than anything, I wanted to. I just... I don't know what was wrong with me."

This is so painful. He sounds like a wounded little boy. I don't know how it's possible, but I'm beginning to feel a pang of sympathy for him. His voice still sounds as kind as it did the first time I heard it—the first time it deceived me. I press my face into my hands, hating myself for pitying him.

Grayson sits silently outside my door for a few minutes before speaking again. "I couldn't control myself," Grayson says softly. "You were just so beautiful, sitting there on the stairs like a broken angel. I needed to touch you to see that you were real. And once I started touching you, I couldn't seem to stop. I felt like you might disappear right before my eyes. I needed to have you, while you were still here on this earth, in human form. I couldn't waste a second not being inside you. I needed to drown in your beauty; I needed to feel you around me. I needed to feel every inch of you, whether you would have me or

CLARITY 2

not." His voice has been growing quieter until it is a barely audible whisper. He pauses to take a deep, mournful breath.

"I felt like I could fuck you into being real. I felt like I could fuck you into being mine."

I am so horrified that I do not know how to respond. I wrap my arms around myself and double over, trying to push his voice out of my mind.

"You were an angel," Grayson says again. "I was guiding you through the halls, and staring at you. And I just started getting more and more... excited. I thought that if I could just have you once, just one taste—that it would somehow be everything I ever needed."

I am struggling to breathe. I am struggling to think. My lips are parted in shock and disbelief. "I was never an angel," I say dumbly, because it is the only thing I can manage to say. "I was just a girl."

"You were so much more than a girl," Grayson says with complete certainty. "Maybe you didn't even know, but I could see it. And I just couldn't wait. I couldn't stand the thought of you rejecting me. I don't know what came over me, but even your hand on my arm... I couldn't bear it. I needed you. Right then and there. I needed to have you. You understand, don't you? I needed you, Helen. I needed you."

I find myself breathing very rapidly, as

though I have just finished running a small marathon. I lift my fingers to plug my ears to drown out the sound. This can't be real. This can't be happening. His voice is so soft that my fingers actually do manage to muffle him completely, but once I am unable to hear anything, I begin to panic. I am already so oblivious to my surroundings. He could use a ladder to climb in the window, and I wouldn't even hear it. He could have found a secret entrance to my room and be standing in front of me right now, and I wouldn't even know. I rip my fingers out of my ears to keep from sending myself into a panic. Of course, he is still talking.

"... went to counseling with her. Your sister thinks there's something wrong with me. Sex addiction, or something of the sort. But I think she's wrong, Helen. It's just you. It's just the thought of you that makes me feel this way. Don't get me wrong, I grew to love Carmen over the years. But I only started seeing her because I saw a tiny bit of your spark in her." He sighs. "Don't you understand? Fucking her was the closest I could get to having you again."

"Oh my god," I moan in horror. "Please stop. Stop. Stop."

"You need to hear this," Grayson insists. "I was so disappointed when you stopped going to school. You even left your dorm. You headed back here, to your home. And I followed you. I watched

CLARITY 2

you, and I was waiting for an opportunity to see you again. To touch you again. To taste you again. But somehow, you escaped me. You disappeared, and I needed to find you. That's why I first spoke to Carmen. To find out where you were. She had no idea, and I was heartbroken. But Carmen wasn't like you. She was friendly, flirtatious, and she expressed interest in me. At first, I was too upset over losing you to consider dating her, but as time went on, and my wounds healed... Carmen became my consolation prize."

"I wish I didn't have to hear any of this," I say miserably. "I need to go back in time and unhear everything I just heard."

"I'm glad you're home, Helen," Grayson says quietly. "I do love your sister, but I was thinking that we could work out an arrangement of sorts. I want to see you sometimes. When Carmen is away from home, or busy at work—I want to be with you. I need this. We're family now, so you'll help me out, right? I want to see you on the side. I want you to be my mistress."

I finally snap. I finally start laughing hysterically. My laughter sounds zany and bizarre. I allow my body to fall to the side until I am lying on the ground and clutching my stomach and laughing. I have completely cracked. I am laughing so hard that I almost don't notice my phone ringing.

"Is that your boyfriend, Helen?" Grayson

asks angrily. "That fucking jerk who was here at the wedding? Don't answer it. Forget about him. I'll fucking kill him."

I slam my fist into the dresser which is blocking my door. This time I am filled with aggression and fury. "Maybe I'll kill you instead," I tell Grayson in a cheerful voice. "You've driven me insane. Doesn't that make me the dangerous one?" I am just talking out of my ass, but it feels good to turn the threatening around on him. I am sick of being the victim.

Placing my palm on the ground, I push myself off the ground and move across the room to answer my phone. "Hello?" I say in an upbeat tone.

"Winter?" Liam says. "Hey! So I had some questions I wanted to ask about our date tomorrow..."

I suddenly frown. "One sec." Holding the phone against my ear, I move over to my closet and open the doors. I move inside and shut the doors, and position my body between rows of hanging dresses to conceal my voice. "What's up?"

"Well, I have some really awesome ideas of things we could do after the appointment. Owen's been helping me with something he calls 'The Ultimate List of Best First Dates.' I know, that sounds ridiculous, but I was actually surprised to see that he had some really great ideas! They're

CLARITY 2

not all even based on porn. I tried to incorporate them with my own, and..."

The frown on my face has been growing deeper and deeper the entire time that Liam has been speaking. "Look," I tell him in a snappish tone. "I'm going to have to cancel."

"What? Why?"

"Because Grayson is harassing me, and I can't deal with this," I say angrily. "Liam, I'm sorry. I can't stay here another day. I want to go home. I'm going to pack my suitcase and wait until he goes to sleep, and get the hell out of here. I need to leave. ASAP."

"Don't." Liam says the word softly, and then he sighs. "Okay. Just give me an hour. I'll come and rescue you from your tower, and the fearsome ogre. We'll do our date today instead of tomorrow. I have a strategy. I'm sure I can make you feel better. What do you say?"

"No," I say firmly. "I don't want to leave my room. Not unless it's to leave for good."

"Just trust me, Winter. You said you'd trust me," Liam says forcefully. "Please."

"You can't come here," I say with concern. "He said he'd kill you. He has a gun, remember?"

"I'm not afraid of a coward like Grayson," Liam says urgently. "Come on. I am sure that if you go on this date with me, you'll feel better about everything. It will change your life. I promise. Please give me a chance?"

Loretta Lost

"And if it doesn't change my life," I tell him softly. "You'll take me home to New Hampshire?"

"It's a deal," he agrees. "Put on a sports bra and some comfortable clothes. As though we were going on a jog."

"A sports bra?" I say in surprise.

"Just trust me," he repeats solemnly. "No asking questions—just do as I say."

"Fine," I say grumpily, hanging up the phone. Even as intelligent as Liam is, I highly doubt that he can magically change my life with a single date and a sports bra. Still, some part of me really wants him to, and dearly hopes he can.

CLARITY 2

Chapter Six

Getting out of the house was a great idea. I am sitting in the passenger seat of Liam's car, and it is a lot nicer than Owen's old vehicle. The seats are ultra-cushiony, and the leathery smell is soothing. The car drives a lot smoother too, and I feel fewer of the bumps and potholes on the road. It is very relaxing.

The best part is that Grayson isn't in the car. And with each passing mile, he is farther and farther away. I do feel free and liberated—like a princess rescued from an ogre. Even if Liam's planned date fails to change my life, I still appreciate that he forced me to get out of the house. I feel like myself again.

"We're almost there," Liam tells me. "Now you might think this is weird at first, but just trust me and go with it."

"Should I be worried?" I ask him with a quizzical smile.

"Nope. You should be delirious with excitement."

Loretta Lost

I snort at this. "You sure are confident."

"No one is *ever* disappointed with my surprises," Liam assures me.

"Maybe I'll be the first," I say, making a face. "I barely know you! This could be awful. You could be taking me to... a hypnotist. You could be trying to change my life by erasing all my bad memories. And when hypnotizing me fails, you could give me a lobotomy or something. What if you're actually a crazy mad-scientist type of doctor?"

Liam laughs as he parks the car. "With an imagination like that, I can see why you write such excellent books. Don't worry, I'm not going to erase your memory. Wait there for a sec." He turns off the engine of the car, and exits the vehicle.

A moment later, I hear the sound of him opening my car door. I smile at this, and unbuckle my seatbelt before stepping out. "Where are we?" I ask, trying to identify our location through listening to the street sounds.

"No asking questions," he says in a teasing voice. "It might ruin the surprise. Do you want to take my elbow?"

"Sure," I say cautiously, reaching out to circle my hand around his upper arm. He guides me slowly and carefully toward a building, and opens a door. Once we step through it, he places my hand on a railing.

"There's a narrow staircase here," he tells

CLARITY 2

me, as he begins to climb the flight of stairs.

I climb behind him until we reach a landing. Once we are there, I feel that the material on the ground has changed. It's rubbery.

"Take off your shoes," Liam tells me, "and hand me your jacket."

Smiling to mask my confusion, I comply with his commands. I can hear him removing his shoes as well. He gives me his elbow again, and guides me through another set of doors. I am surprised to feel that the ground has grown quite soft beneath my feet, which are now only clad in a pair of socks. I am even more surprised when I feel Liam stopping and bowing deeply.

"Liam!" says an older man's voice with a hearty laugh. "Shame on you for getting me out of bed this early for an 'emergency session.' Where's the fire, son?"

"I'm sorry, Sensei," Liam says respectfully. "I would like you to meet Winter, the girl I told you about on the phone."

"Ah, a lovely fire indeed," says the older man. "I'm James. Nice to meet you, Winter."

"Hello," I say shyly.

"James has been my judo teacher since I was a kid," Liam explains to me. "He's the best. He's also partially blind."

"Judo?" I whisper in surprise. "You want me to learn how to fight?"

"Yes," Liam says, "but it's so much more

than that. I considered taking you to therapy, but you've already studied psychology—they can't tell you anything you don't already know. I believe you need something stronger than counseling."

"Can a blind person really learn how to fight?" I ask in wonder.

James laughs. "Of course! You can ask my blind students who medaled at the Paralympics. The Judo competition is reserved specifically for the visually impaired."

I did not know this. I feel like a door has been opened, and a huge tidal wave of information has gushed through and smacked me in the face. I also do feel excited. Scared, but excited. I am already grateful to Liam for teaching me that there was a possible power that I *could have* that I had never considered exploring.

"I was hoping you could give her a personalized crash course in basic self-defense," Liam tells his instructor. "I think she's a fast learner and will pick it up quickly."

"Sure," James says, "but I think we need to start with the philosophy of the art. You see, Winter, many sighted folks consider us blind people easy targets. Muggings, violence, abuse—you name it. We can often seem disadvantaged and defenseless, and that encourages attacks against us. The solution? Well, we need both to stop *seeming* defenseless, and to stop *being* defenseless."

"How do we do that?" I ask him curiously.

CLARITY 2

"You need to learn how to carry yourself," James tells me, and I hear his voice moving closer. "Sighted people can use body language to convey a sense of confidence and strength. This automatically wards off many attackers. However, body language is learned through visually observing the postures of others. I will be teaching you how to be strong and aggressive in your stance."

I nod, for this makes a lot of sense. "I would like to learn."

"If you're going to study under me, the number one rule is that you should not be afraid of touch." The teacher's voice is calm and pleasant, and I am eager to absorb his every word. "If someone tries to grab you or hit you, then they are stepping onto *your* battlefield. Your body is your turf—and the moment someone steps onto *your* turf, you are no longer blind. If they touch you, you touch them back. You grab whatever you can. If you can *feel* your attacker, you can *see* your attacker."

"Okay," I say softly.

"Do you see this?" James reaches out to touch my shoulder. "Now you know exactly where I am. Now you have valuable information about me—all the information you need to take me down."

I nod in understanding.

"And now—observe this," James says

removing his hand from my shoulder. He steps around me, slowly circling my body. "Now that I am no longer touching you, I have become invisible to you. I could be anywhere around you. You have some clues, but not all the clues you need. You don't want to run away. You don't want more space between us. You want to move *into* me so that you can *see* my body and neutralize it so that it is no longer a threat. It might seem counterintuitive at first, but you'll soon understand once we begin training."

My mind is blown. It makes so much sense. When Grayson attacked me, I ran away. I am always getting nervous and flinching away from contact with people. I never realized that doing so gave *them* the power.

"Remember this concept," James says again. "If they're not touching you, they're invisible. So take advantage of touch, and make it your friend—not your enemy."

I take a deep breath and nod thankfully. "I will," I say with determination. It also occurs to me that I have psychological issues with running away. Going to New Hampshire might have saved my skin for the time being, but it did not erase my problems completely. Instead, it exposed my home to infiltration from my attacker. If I had stayed, and pushed forward instead of caving in, I could have changed everything.

I want to change everything.

CLARITY 2

"It's good to keep your enemies close," Liam tells me, "so don't worry. We'll teach you what you need to do."

"And I have the perfect way to start!" James says happily. "Winter, how would you like to kick Liam's ass a lot?"

A laugh bubbles out of my throat. "Really? I think I'd love that."

"Darn," Liam says in dismay.

The teacher gets to work on showing me what to do if someone has placed a hand around my neck. He shows me where to place my thumb and how to twist my opponents arm until he is disabled. He shows me how to follow through until my opponent is on the ground. He has me try it gently a few times in slow-motion before turning to Liam.

"Alright, son," James says cheerfully. "I want you to grab Winter by the throat."

Liam hesitates. "Do you feel comfortable with that?" he asks me.

"Just shut up and do it already," I say with a smile. "I want to try this."

"Okay, here goes," he says, before reaching for my neck.

For a moment, I do feel a bit of fear. I do remember Grayson's hand on my neck. For only a fraction of a second, as his hand comes into contact with my skin, I am paralyzed in terror. Then, as his hand clamps around my neck, I remember that he is now 'visible' to me. Comforted by the fact that this is a safe environment, and I have simple instructions, I grab his hand and twist it until Liam is on the ground, and my body is positioned over his, pinning him down.

Liam laughs. "Ouch! I knew you'd be a fast learner. That was almost perfect, and it was only your first try."

I blush in embarrassment when I realize how close my body is to his, and I begin to pull away.

"No," James says, placing a hand on my back. "Touch is your weapon, remember? You want to move your knees closer to his body. If you pull away, he'll get free and attack you again. Remember, you are not only blind, but you are a woman. Which means you will be much smaller than most of your opponents. Although you may not weigh much, if you position your body correctly, you can overpower someone who weighs twice as much as you do. Really *press* your body down on his and *lock* him down. Knees and arms closer! Closer!"

"Okay," I say nervously, pushing aside my modesty and focusing on the technique. "Like this?"

"Yes! Yes! That's it," James says. "Now, Liam, try to break free."

Liam struggles against me, and I hold my position fast. A few times, he nearly breaks my

CLARITY 2

hold and I am worried that I'm doing it wrong. After a few seconds of struggling, he gives up.

"I'm down," Liam says in approval. "She's got me."

"Great," says James. "Now let's move on to the next technique."

The rest of the lesson passes by in a whirlwind of energy and struggling to achieve perfection. I feel so honored by the way that James and Liam treat me; like I am truly capable of doing this. It really does strengthen my confidence in myself, and makes me want to try to do more and more. My muscles quickly begin to ache, having not been used very much in years. However, I welcome the feeling and push onward, feeling exhilarated from the exercise and motion.

I feel like Liam has dumped me into a swift-moving river and demanded that I swim. I love it. I love the challenge, and I love being immersed in fast-paced new information. It's intimidating, and it could certainly drown me, but I won't be tugged under by the current. I'm going to swim.

Chapter Seven

"You were really good," Liam says as he drives me home. "Are you sure you've never done any martial arts before?"

"No," I say with a laugh, "I haven't. Unless you count years of wrestling with my sister—almost every day, for every tiny thing. Even when I first came home, we got physical a few times."

"That must be it. The source of your great talent," Liam says solemnly.

"Don't be ridiculous," I tell him, but I *am* really happy about my performance.

Snapping his fingers, Liam makes an excited exclamation. "Oh! I have an idea. Let's delay your surgery so you can be blind enough to compete in the Paralympics. What do you say? You just have to train really hard, then we can head to Rio de Janeiro for 2016. I was just going to watch it from TV, but being there would be so much better. And James can add your picture to his impressive wall of successful students."

"Are you joking?" I ask him incredulously.

CLARITY 2

"Nope."

"Liam!" I burst into laughter.

"What?" he asks in a wounded tone. "What's so funny?"

"I just had my first lesson today. Cool your balls, buddy."

"My balls are... at the perfectly appropriate temperature," he assures me. "I'm just thinking of the possibilities!"

I growl at him softly. "Are you my pimp now, or am I a dancing circus animal?"

"Can't it be both?" he asks whimsically.

"I know you're just trying to make me feel better," I tell him, "and it's working. Just remember that I'm learning to fight to stay alive and protect my sister, not for the glamor of showing off my smooth moves on TV."

"Can't you do both?" he asks glumly.

I can't help smiling at his attitude. Liam is possibly one of the most positive people I've ever met. His enthusiasm is apparent in everything he does—it is obvious that he's very passionate about both judo, and his job. Being around him makes me feel like anything is possible. "Even though you're insane," I tell him, "and you push me around way too much—I still think you're sweet."

"I solemnly vow that whenever I manipulate you, I will always have your best interests at heart," Liam says with complete seriousness.

"Wow," I say in mock admiration. "That was

really romantic. I need to save those words." I pull out my phone and press my thumb down on the solitary circular button, and request that it make a recording. Then I repeat his words into the machine: "I solemnly vow that whenever I manipulate you, I will always have your best interests at heart."

He laughs at this. "Why are you recording that? Are you going to use it in one of your books?"

"Maybe," I say teasingly, "but also, if this dating thing works out? You can use it in your wedding vows."

"No way," Liam says. "My wedding vows would be so much more interesting than that."

"Like what?" I ask with a challenge in my voice.

"Hmm," he says thoughtfully. "Like... 'I vow to love you so much that I will always let you choose what we watch together on TV. If I don't like what you're watching, I'm just going to go watch my own thing in a different room anyway.'"

"Really, really romantic," I say in amusement.

"Also," he adds, picking up momentum, "this one's really good: 'I vow always to leave the last potato chip for you. But it's the only one you're getting, because I call dibs on the rest of the bag.'"

He finally manages to get a real laugh out of me. I have to catch myself to try and stop from

CLARITY 2

laughing too loudly. I have been holding this in for some time and trying to appear cool and sardonic, but now he's definitely won. I can't help relaxing a little. "I envy the lucky lady who gets to tie the knot with you," I tell him with a grin.

"I can be a regular Casanova," he assures me. "I picked up a lot from watching Owen over the years. For example, the date we just had? The truth is that I just chose this because it involved a *lot* of physical contact. I'm pretty sure we got to third base there. I got to cop a lot of feels."

I twist my face up in what I imagine must be a skeptical look.

"Winter, what are you giving me that look for?"

"I highly doubt that *this* was on Owen's list of ultimate first dates."

"Maybe it was," Liam says.

"No," I tell him. "It was special and meaningful, and you chose it specifically for me. I won't let you cheapen it with jokes. It was amazing."

Liam's voice lowers a little. "Did you really like it?"

"Yes," I respond sincerely. "It was a lot of fun. It was also just what I needed. You didn't just help me. You helped me help myself, which is far more valuable. I can't thank you enough."

"You're very welcome," he responds, "but you're not a master yet. We'll have to keep training, and keep going back, dozens of times."

The idea of more training gives me a thrill. I am somehow bursting with energy—even though I have spent much more energy today than I would on an average day, I seem to have more because of this. It's ironic and puzzling, but I love the sensation.

"When can we do this again?" I ask him shyly.

"Soon," he responds instantly. "Let's make a promise that we'll train with James at least three times a week, for a minimum of two hours. Even if things don't work out with us—we'll just quit going there on dates and go as friends. It's important to do this. It will change your life."

"You already have changed my life," I tell him softly. I think about where I was earlier today, sitting with my back to a dresser and feeling terrified of a door opening. I think about where I have been for several days, confined to my room and unable to get out of bed. Unable to do any work. Unable to think of anything other than my overwhelming fear. I know that I probably don't know enough about judo yet to actually stand a chance in a fight, but I feel like I have broken through some barrier today. I am not afraid anymore. Tears spring to my eyes, but they are tears of happiness. "Liam," I say, and my voice is all choked up. However, having learned that touch can be my friend, I decide not to speak and simply

CLARITY 2

reach out and place my hand on his leg. I place a gentle pressure on his thigh to try and convey my gratitude.

He removes one of his hands from the steering wheel, and places it over my own. He interlaces his fingers with mine, in a gesture which clearly conveys him accepting my sentiments.

The touch is so powerful that there really is no need for speech.

A few more minutes and miles pass, and our fingers remain woven together. It is so comforting and natural, and I wish that the moment would last forever. I feel like my skin just melts together with his, and disappears into his body. It is like his hand belongs attached to mine—like it always had been there before, but was separated for this lifetime, and only just reunited.

He feels like the missing part of me that I never even realized I was missing. I never thought I could feel so secure and complete. I don't know how I'm going to rip myself away from him. All I can seem to think about is how I *need* to be even closer to him than this. I want to be around him all the time—I want to spend as much time with him as possible. He makes me feel like life could be a good thing. He makes me laugh, even when I'm trying to be standoffish and snobby. He easily breaks down all my walls with his gentle persistence. He believes I can do anything, and makes me into a better version of myself. He helps me to see the things I cannot see. He makes me feel fulfilled.

"We're almost at your place," he says quietly.

There is a silence, and we both seem to feel the ache of the impending loss. However, as he continues to drive onward, my thoughts begin to focus less on how incredible Liam is, and more on the horrible hellhole that is looming in the distance. I have been enjoying myself so much that I had almost entirely forgotten about Grayson. I had forgotten how soon I would be thrust back into the same dwelling with him. I had forgotten that date had to end. I had forgotten how quickly we were approaching my house.

"We're here," Liam says, as he removes his hand from mine and begins to turn the steering wheel.

His words are like a slap in my face. I am seized with a great panic and I reach out to grab his wrist to halt the turning. "No. No, please." I take a few quick breaths. "Liam, I'm not ready to go back in there. Can we just drive around for a little? Just a little more?"

"Sure," he says, without hesitation. He pulls back onto the road and begins driving again.

"I'm sorry," I tell him. "I just couldn't—I need a minute to prepare."

"It's okay," Liam says. He hesitates before speaking. "I'm really not supposed to do this—it

CLARITY 2

could present problems for my job. But if you really want, you could stay at my place. It's very small, but I could take the couch..."

"No, no," I say softly. "I appreciate the offer, but I don't want to impose. You've already done so much for me. I just need a few minutes to gather my strength."

"Would you like a distraction?" Liam asks.

"What do you mean?" I ask him. I am surprised when he pulls the car over sharply into the shoulder.

He parks the car and unlocks his seatbelt before leaning across the center console to place his face near mine. He slides his hand along my neck, just under my ear. His thumb rests lightly on my earlobe. "May I?" he breathes.

I cannot find the words, so I force myself to nod.

Liam presses his lips against mine with a soft and tender pressure. At first, the kiss is barely a whisper of a touch, as though I am fragile and made of glass that might shatter. Once my surprise eases away, and I am able to respond, he notices this and begins to deepen the kiss. His hand slips around the back of my head, and his lips become more intense and demanding.

I find myself swept away in the sensation. His touch is so strong and forceful, yet filled with sweetness and compassion. He seems to have discovered that I am not fragile glass, but a real woman made of flesh and blood—and he treats me accordingly. I kiss back ardently, eager to lose myself in the loveliness of the connection.

I can taste a little bit of masculine sweat lingering on his skin from our earlier workout. It is salty and pleasant, and with a bit of a spicy flavor. I can also smell the muskiness of cologne on his jacket. I am just beginning to relax and pour all of my pent-up emotion into the kiss when he pulls away.

He clears his throat, and speaks in a husky voice. "I had better take you home."

"Yes," I say quietly, in disappointment. I lower my chin and try to catch my breath as my heartbeat races—for the first time in forever, I have butterflies in my stomach from an emotion other than fear. "When can we do that again?" I ask him, trying to conceal my desperation. I want to see him again so badly.

"Soon," he says with an upbeat tone. "Maybe next time we can go on a true Owen-style date."

"I can't wait," I tell him with a smile.

CLARITY 2

Chapter Eight

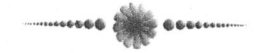

"You're underweight," Dr. Howard accuses me. "Before you get your eye surgery, I'm going to recommend you gain at least ten pounds."

"Ten pounds!" I repeat in dismay as I step off the scale. "But I feel fine. Maybe this is just a good weight for me."

"As you currently are, you may experience slower wound healing," Dr. Howard says. "It's safer if you gain a little weight."

"Well, I've begun working out a little," I tell her as I return to my seat. "I've begun going to judo classes. So I might gain some muscle."

"That's great, honey. But you need to *eat*. A lot."

I think about the situation at home where I need to stockpile non-perishables in my room to avoid running into Grayson. If I felt my comfortable going into the rest of the house, I could happily eat a dozen cupcakes every day and fatten myself up.

"Dr. Larson told me that you haven't eaten

real food in years," Dr. Howard says, tapping her pen on her folder. "So I'd like to get some blood work done and determine if you have any deficiencies."

"Okay, Leslie."

I hear the flipping of paper as she closes my file. "So you've begun dating Liam?" she asks me curiously.

I suddenly feel embarrassed. I remember that Carmen had mentioned that Liam and Leslie seemed close at the wedding. Am I stepping on her toes? "Uh, yes," I tell her nervously. "Do you think it's a bad idea?"

"Not at all!" Leslie says with enthusiasm. "Remember, I'm the one who gave him your books in the first place and recommended he take you on as a patient. He's always been a really sensitive guy—really interested in improving every aspect of his patients' lives, not just their eyes. I thought you two would get along."

"And *you* don't have any... interest in him?" I ask her awkwardly.

"Good grief, Helen!" Leslie says with a laugh. "Just because my husband is dead doesn't mean I'm going to go rob the cradle. I'm nearly twice that boy's age."

"I was just curious," I tell her. "I feel like Liam's too good to be true, and there must be something wrong here. Is there? Is really... a good guy?"

CLARITY 2

"He's the best guy," Dr. Howard says without hesitation. Then she pauses. "But you should still be careful, Helen. Don't rush into things too quickly."

"I'm not," I assure her. "That's why I'm asking your opinion."

"You might be a little eager to fall for him, considering you've been isolated for so long. Especially with your past, Liam must seem like the best thing since sliced bread. Just try to be cautious and logical." Leslie sighs. "I suppose that since your mom is gone, I feel the need to give you motherly advice. Even the best of men have huge flaws. They need to be... worked on."

"What does that mean?" I ask her.

"Oh, I don't know," she says. "Just ignore me; I like to ramble!"

"No, Leslie. Please tell me."

The doctor begins tapping her pen on her desk. "It's just that you young girls seem to think that relationships are all rainbows and butterflies all the time. Back in my day, when we had a problem with our men, we just made it work. No matter what. Even your mother—she was upset for years about the way your dad didn't take care of himself. Richard was a very heavy smoker. But Meredith didn't leave him and go off in search of greener grass. She just made him stop." Leslie stands up and moves to the other end of the small room. "Your mom refused to have kids with

Loretta Lost

Richard unless he promised to seriously begin fixing his health so he'd be around to see you girls grow up—to be there for your graduation and weddings. It's a good thing she made him promise that—none of us had any idea that *she* would be the one who wasn't around."

"Yeah," I say softly. "Why are you telling me this?"

"I'm just thinking about Carmen, the poor girl," says Leslie with a sigh. "She's been coming in for checkups since she got pregnant, and really flying off the handle. Do you want to know what she said a few months ago? 'Please tell me there's something wrong with the baby so I can get an abortion and don't have to marry that bastard.' I couldn't believe my ears. Why would she say something like that? Grayson seems like a perfectly nice guy. Even Richard loves him. They seemed really happy at their wedding."

I groan and lower my face into my hands. "She said that?"

"Yes. Right when she found out she was pregnant. I think it was shock or something. I better not ever hear you speaking about Liam that way, young lady. If something goes wrong—and it will—just stick it out and fix it, okay? He's a gem. Don't toss him into the trash heap if you find one tiny flaw in the jewel."

I press my fingers into my aching temples. This is about as much motherly advice as I can

CLARITY 2

handle. It does make me wonder what our actual mother would have said about the situation with Grayson. She was pretty close to Dr. Howard, and she might have had a similar opinion. Somehow, I feel that we never would have gotten into this situation at all if we hadn't lost Mom. We all just seemed to fall apart without her. "Thanks for the checkup, Leslie," I tell her, "and thanks for the chat. I'd better get going now."

Dr. Howard snaps her fingers. "I nearly forgot. You should get a pap smear."

"No way!" I shout. "I don't need one."

"Helen. Your mother had pre-cancerous cells on her cervix. You're getting a pap smear."

"Yes, but it's not what killed her. She just got a hysterectomy and she was fine."

"Thanks to *my* early detection," Dr. Howard argues. "Look, it's just a basic screening test. I know it's uncomfortable, but you haven't had one in years. We need to do a complete physical."

"Can we do it later?" I grumble. "Liam is going to be poking giant needles into my eyes, along with a huge tube for a camera, and possibly other things. I'm going to have enough strange objects being shoved into my body soon enough—can we just skip the pap?"

"No," Leslie says, growing impatient. "This is important. Helen, you're dating a doctor. How about I call Liam and tell him you're refusing to have a pap done?"

Loretta Lost

"No, no, no!" I say, lifting both of my hands anxiously. "Don't tell him about that. This is super personal and intimate..."

"Poking needles into your eyes is as intimate as it gets," Dr. Howard says teasingly. "It's a level of trust that most couples will never need to reach; an activity most will never share!"

"Leslie!"

"Fine, I won't call Liam since you don't seem to enjoy the idea of having your cervix discussed with him. I'll call your father."

I drop both of my hands to my sides in defeat. "Fine," I say weakly. "Do the damn test."

CLARITY 2

Chapter Nine

A few days later...

"I have something planned that will blow your mind," Liam says while giving me a hug in greeting.

I no longer doubt his ability to blow my mind. I gingerly return his hug and rest my cheek on the lapel of his coat for a second. "Thank you for trying to make every day so special for me," I tell him softly.

"Hey, it's my pleasure! I love surprising you," he says in an upbeat tone. He takes my arm to guide me to his car, and opens the door for me. "And here's the first surprise of the day! I promised you a true Owen-style date, but I bet you didn't expect it to actually include *Owen*."

"Yo," says the cheerful doctor from the backseat of the vehicle. "What's up, Winter?"

"Hi Owen," I say pleasantly as I climb into

Loretta Lost

the passenger seat. When Liam closes the door and begins walking around the vehicle, I turn back to Owen with a smile. "What are you doing here? Should I be worried?"

"Naw," Owen says with a drawl. "Liam was afraid that he had used up all his best topics of conversation. He has maybe three subjects tops that he can speak about without boring everyone to sleep and sounding like an idiot. So he got me to come along to be his wingman—it's my job to act really dumb so he will seem way smarter in comparison."

"That's not the reason at all," Liam protests as he climbs into the driver's seat. "I just wanted to demonstrate my smooth social skills to impress Winter. Have you introduced her to Caroline yet?"

I have noticed the additional person sitting in the backseat, even though her breathing is very quiet and she hasn't spoken. I am curious, but I didn't want to ask.

"This is my lady-love," Owen says proudly. "The gorgeous, enchanting, and very flexible Caroline."

"For god's sake, Owen," Caroline mutters angrily. "Why do you have to introduce me like that? What if I introduced you to people as 'the dorky man-child who only thinks with his penis and barely survived med school'? How would you like that?"

"It would be accurate," Owen says in

CLARITY 2

confusion. "But I'd appreciate if you added something about my stamina in there. Maybe a little compliment on my girth? You have to highlight my positive attributes."

Caroline releases a stream of furiously-spoken words in a foreign language.

"Is that German?" I ask nervously.

"She just insulted my manhood," Owen explains, "and called me a bunch of names I'd rather not translate. I bet she just wants me to kiss her to keep her filthy mouth shut."

"You pig," Caroline says, but in the next moment she unbuckles her seat belt and moves over to sit on Owen's lap. Soon, the two are lip-locked and there are sounds of a passionate make-out session coming from the back seat.

"Um. Did I miss something?" I ask Liam, screwing up my face in confusion.

"Don't look at me," he says as he starts the car, "I don't understand those two in the least. Owen! Do whatever you want back there, just don't get my seats dirty!"

"Aye, aye, Cap'n!" Owen responds.

"It's nice to meet you, Winter," Caroline says elegantly, as though she had not just been shoving her tongue down Owen's throat.

"Uh, it's great to meet you, Caroline," I say, trying to hide my shock at their behavior.

"You'll get used to it," Liam assures me as he drives away from my house. "And if you don't,

Loretta Lost

at least I'll seem like a much more civilized and cultured human being than those two animals in the backseat."

"I resent that!" Owen says between bouts of loud, amorous lip-smacking.

I listen to them for a few minutes before a grin breaks out on my face. I shake my head in amusement.

Liam reaches over and pats my leg. "If it really bothers you, we can make Owen drive on the way home and we can torture them with our own gross tonsil-tango."

"That sounds lovely," I tell him. My shoulders shake in a small giggle. "Disgusting, but lovely."

Liam drives for a few minutes before he starts to slow down. "This is interesting, Winter. The GPS just made me turn down a street I don't know. I don't come to your neighborhood often—I didn't know you had all these adorable little art shops!"

"Yes," I say with a smile. "Many of the locals are obsessed with decorating their homes with the perfect paintings and potteries and..."

"Antiques!" Liam exclaims, slamming on the brakes.

My body is propelled forward slightly before being rammed back into his cushiony leather seats. I hear Caroline giggle as her body is thrust against Owen's. "Antiques?" I repeat in confusion. "Is this

CLARITY 2

where we're going?"

"No," Liam says cryptically. "Just a quick pit stop. Wait here!"

The car swerves sharply as he pulls into the parking lot and swiftly exits the vehicle. He even leaves the car running.

"Okay," I say slowly. "What's happening here? What did I miss?"

"Liam likes old things," Owen explains when he can manage to pull his mouth away from Caroline for a moment.

"Old things?" I ask again.

"He collects antiques," Caroline explains. "You should see his apartment. Very small, but very stylish. Everything artsy, everything vintage."

"To be honest, I thought he was gay for a little while," Owen admits. "It seems unnatural for any straight man to like funky furniture as much as he does."

I smile at this. I like the fact that Liam has an artistic side. Still, I am a bit confused. "You thought he was gay?" I ask Owen. "Hasn't he dated many women?"

"Very rarely. Too rarely. It takes a lot for him to find a woman interesting. He's too picky," Owen explains.

"It's the story," Caroline says softly. "The man likes old furniture because it has a history. He can touch the wood, and it tells him a beautiful tale of love and loss. He likes his women the same

Loretta Lost

way; vastly complex with endless layers and depth. He wants to look into her eyes and see a touch of tragedy and the promise of victory."

"Wow, Caroline," Owen says in amazement. "That's astute. Hey, I have refined tastes too. I like my women to be... female."

Caroline curses again in German before slapping Owen in the face.

"I'm kidding!" Owen whines. "Relax, baby. You know I love how fierce and fiery you are. Come here. Bring it home for Papa."

"Whoa," I say in discomfort, feeling like I am intruding on a very private moment. The sound of incessant lip-smacking is less tolerable now that Liam has stepped out of the car. "Does anyone know where we're going?"

"He said that he needs to fatten you up before your eye surgery," Owen says, groaning as Caroline makes noises that indicate she might be nibbling his neck. "So we're going to some fancy-schmancy food thing."

"Food thing?" I ask, pressuring the pair for details.

"It's a wine and cheese party," Caroline explains. "I could not refuse free booze—it will help me forget that I've wasted five years of my life dating a boy who will never grow into a man."

"Hey!" Owen says in a wounded tone. "It will also help me forget that I'm dating a B-cup who won't get implants or let me try her back

CLARITY 2

door."

"Too much information," I tell the couple, "too much information!"

"I think he mentioned a competition too," Caroline says. "Something about a blind tasting?"

"A blind wine tasting competition?" I say very loudly. "Are you kidding me? Really!" Just as I say this, struggling very hard not to squeal in excitement, Liam opens his car door.

"Darn," he says in disappointment. "You two ruined my surprise."

"Liam!" I exclaim, grabbing his sleeve. "Really? A wine tasting competition?!"

"Yes," he says with a laugh. "When I first met you, you were hugging a bottle of Cabernet Sauvignon from the Napa Valley pretty tightly. Remember how I asked for a sip? That was some good stuff. I was impressed. I thought we could test your mettle and see whether you have a good palate for identifying wines from all over the world."

"Of *course* I do!" I tell him with excitement. "My mom and dad used to take me to wine tasting parties all the time when I was a teenager. They used to show off my skill. It was totally illegal for me to be drinking, so I just swirled it around on my tongue and spit it out—I felt so grown up and sophisticated. I can tell you what anything is. *Anything!*"

"I was hoping you'd get excited about this,"

he says with pleasure. "I just didn't think you'd get *this* excited! If you're half as good as you say you are, I'm going to have to bet money on you."

"I wish Owen would do something nice like that for me," Caroline says with disappointment and envy.

Owen ignores her, leaning forward. I can tell because his voice gets closer, and his breath tickles my ear. "Hey, Liam," he says curiously. "What's in the bag, bro?"

"Dammit. Why do you keep ruining my surprises?" Liam snaps at his friend.

"Oh no," Owen groans. "Don't tell me you brought more fruity antiques."

"Fruity?" Liam says in dismay. "Is that what he's been saying about me? None of my antiques are fruity in any way!"

"What's in the bag?" Caroline echoes. "Show it to us, Liam."

"Alright," Liam mutters. "You bunch of spoilsports. It's a gift for Winter." He reaches into the cloth bag and begins unwrapping an item that has been tightly wound in wrapping paper. He then places the item in my hands.

I am surprised by the heft of the object. There seems to be an ornate and slender handle which leads up to an oval frame. I run my hands over the center of the object and discover a smooth surface. "Is it a... mirror?" I ask him.

"Yes," he tells me, reaching over to brush a

CLARITY 2

few wisps of hair behind my ear. He leans over and places a kiss on my shoulder. "And soon, you'll be able to see your reflection in it. Then, you can finally discover every aspect of how amazing you are."

I stare down at the object in my hands, and squint as though I might already be able to see a tiny beam or flicker of light reflecting off its surface. Of course, there is nothing. Is it possible that I might actually be able to see into this mirror soon? "Stop getting my hopes up," I tell Liam softly. "Thank you for the gift, but you're being *way* too optimistic."

"Give the boy a break," Caroline says gently. "He's completely smitten with you, Winter. It's adorable."

"What if the operation doesn't work?" I ask them as I lift up the mirror and stare into it with determination, as though I must be able to see if I try hard enough. "What if I can never see *anything* reflected in this mirror?"

"I'll make sure you do," Liam says. "Besides, I won't be working alone. Owen will help me! I know he seems like a dolt, but he's actually really brilliant. There's no one I'd rather have beside me at the operating table."

"Gee," Owen says. He turns to Caroline and speaks in a hushed whisper. "I better not mess up and poke the needle in the wrong place. That would be awkward."

Loretta Lost

"I heard that," I tell him, "and it's not funny."

A feminine hand rests gently on my shoulder. "Don't worry, Winter," Caroline says in a grave voice. "Owen never has any trouble poking things into the right place."

I clear my throat. "I'm not sure if that's supposed to be reassuring... but thanks."

Liam laughs. "Alright, you crazy people. Let's get back on the road. There's a party waiting for us."

As Liam begins to drive away from the antique shop, I continue staring at the ornate mirror in my hand. I can feel the heavy metal object, and I can trace its intricate details, but I can't even see a speck of light illuminating a single corner. It might as well not exist. What if nothing actually exists, and nothing can actually be seen, and it's all some elaborate lie everyone has fabricated to torture me? It's a silly thought, but I often wonder if this darkness is all there really is. Having lived so long with this reality, it's terrifying to think of how great the change would be. How could I accept and adjust to anything else?

I continue to search the obscured mirror for answers as we drive along. What if when I can finally see a girl staring back at me, I don't like what I see? What if she's just another stranger I wish I could escape?

CLARITY 2

Chapter Ten

I gently circle my wrist as it cradles the wine glass, swirling the liquid around to release its aroma. I inhale deeply, allowing the piquant scent to fill my sinuses.

"There's no way she can guess this one," someone in the room whispers.

"Why not?" says Caroline. "She's guessed everything so far."

"But this wine isn't quite so mainstream. I bet she doesn't even get the continent right."

The corner of my lips curl in pleasure at everyone's whispers. Needless to say, I have been able to impress Liam's peers with my vast knowledge of the grape. I have easily beaten out every competitor, which isn't saying much; forced to drink blindfolded from dark glasses, some of the people at the party have been unable to tell red from white. They have made some ridiculous guesses that have caused me to erupt in laughter.

Now, as the sole victor, everyone is continuing to test me to see how far they can strain my knowledge before I break. Liam has been

CLARITY 2

standing off to the side and boasting about me, and I must say that it feels good to be the best at something. Due to my genuine love for wine, it is also quite effortless. It is one of my few hobbies and interests that I kept up with even when I was isolated from society. I still took the time to order a good wine now and then. I would frequently browse the award winning wines for various competitions, and have a few of the more affordable selections sent over to my address. I don't think I could live without the soothing flavors to transport me away on a bad day.

"Well, Winter?" someone prods me. "Are you going to taste it?"

"I bet she has no idea what's in the glass," another person says in a snooty tone.

"You'll bet?" Liam says, and I can hear the sound of him pulling out his wallet. "How much, my friend? A thousand bucks says she gets it spot on."

"Really, Liam? You're nuts. I don't have a thousand dollars on me—but sure. If she gets it, I'll write you a check. If not, you can write me a check."

"Deal," Liam says, shaking his colleague's hand. From what I understand, many of the people at the party are his old college buddies.

"Look at you, Liam," says a woman's voice. "Tossing around your wad. I remember when you were in school, you could barely afford a sandwich."

"That's because I was saving up for my down payment, Alyssa," he tells her.

"Enough suspense!" declares the party host. "Winter, what's your verdict?"

I take another deep whiff of the aroma. "It's red. Vintage. Australia. I'm going to say... South Australia."

"She hasn't even tasted it yet!" someone exclaims in horror.

"Oh, that's right," I say as though I have forgotten. "The taste! That will help me narrow it down." I press my lips against the rim of the glass and tilt it to allow the liquid to seep into my mouth. I swish it around my tongue carefully, allowing the flavor to dance around my taste buds. "Oh, this is very distinctive. You guys are trying to trip me up by using a very small winery, aren't you? It's not going to work. This is from Clare Valley. Specifically, Wakefield Estate." I take another large sip, but this time, just for enjoyment. "2008, Shiraz."

"Fuck," curses the guy who lost his money to Liam.

"Yep. Hand it over, John," Liam says smugly, clapping his hand on his friend's back.

I can hear the other man pull out his checkbook and begin writing, while muttering insults.

"It's not fair to bring a blind girl to a blind

CLARITY 2

tasting, Liam," says a jealous female spectator in the room.

"Why is it not fair?" he asks innocently. "Do you mean to say that it's not fair she is *only* limited to blind tastings? That it's unfair she has never been able to experience the color of various wines? Or to see their stylish bottles and labels?"

"I—I didn't..."

"Sarah, she has no idea what the colors *red* or *white* even mean. Is that fair to her? Do you think her life is easy? Stop discriminating against the disabled!" Liam is obviously slightly drunk and messing with this woman, and I find it hilarious.

"You're right," says the woman meekly. "I'm sorry."

"Hey, wait!" says another person in the room. "It actually might be unfair. Really unfair. I think I recognize this chick." He comes close to me, and looks into my face. "Aren't you Helen Winters? Yeah! Her family owns a whole fucking winery!"

"Is that true?" Owen asks.

"Not exactly," I say in puzzlement. "We sold it years ago. We owned a small private vineyard in Northern Michigan. We made a special ice wine that we called The Winter Grape. My sister and I would spend summers there and help with the cultivation. We never really sold the product commercially, though, so I'm surprised you'd

Loretta Lost

know about us."

"I knew it! Didn't your dad purchase a vineyard out in Long Island last year?" a man insists.

"I don't know," I say in confusion. "Maybe."

"Excuse us for a minute," Liam tells everyone as he places his hand on my back. "Winter and I are going to step out onto the balcony."

"Wait!" says another partygoer, shoving a glass into my hands. "Can you tell what this is, Winter?"

I bring it to my nose and sniff it, and immediately make a face of disgust. "Ugh," I say in displeasure. "You can't expect me to taste this stuff? Is it even wine? It smells like rancid nuts."

Everyone in the room begins to laugh.

"It looks like we've final stumped her," someone says triumphantly.

"Yes, but this doesn't count," another person says. "That wine is sort of a trick question."

"Give me a second," I tell them, wrinkling my nose. I gather my courage and toss the wine down my throat. I scrunch up my eyes and try to avoid gagging on the bitter taste. "That tastes like cat urine," I declare, causing more laughter from the room. When the laughter calms down, I sip the wine again. "But it's actually a 2001 Riesling from Southern Ontario. That horrible taste and smell comes from the fact that the region was invaded by

CLARITY 2

Asian ladybugs around that time. It's a rare wine flaw called ladybug taint. I believe they trashed most of this stuff so it wouldn't be sold."

"Damn," says the party's host, and there is a tone of respect in his voice. "She wins. I give up. I can't stump her."

"Of course, you can't," Liam says as he guides me away from the crowd. "She's too damn good."

I let him lead me out onto the balcony, and I am immediately refreshed by the cool night air. The party is being hosted in a penthouse apartment, and the wind is rather strong; it tosses my hair around my shoulders a little.

"Here," Liam says, pushing a plate toward me that has been sitting out on the patio. "You're supposed to be eating too. You'll never get fat enough for the surgery at this rate."

I feel around on the plate and discover toothpicks shoved into little cubes of cheeses. I pop one in my mouth to try to overpower the taste of the ladybug-tainted wine. "Mmmm. That's nice," I say, taking another piece of cheese.

"You were amazing in there," Liam tells me. He laughs lightly. "I made a few thousand bucks off betting on you."

"I noticed that," I say with a smile. My words feel a bit slow and slurred. "You shamelessly capitalized on my skill—you exploited me for personal gain!"

Loretta Lost

"I hope you don't mind," he says gently. "I don't mean to keep treating you like a circus animal."

"Or like you're my pimp," I add as I pop a few more pieces of cheese into my mouth.

"It's an interesting dynamic," he agrees. "I don't know why things seem to go that way. It might be due to the fact that you're just so good at everything."

"Flattery will get you everywhere," I tell him playfully, poking him in the ribs. I suddenly cast my eyes downward. "Liam, this was a lot of fun."

"It was," he agrees. "Plus, I got to learn fun facts about your past. I knew you loved wine, but I had no idea your family used to own a vineyard!"

"You seem to have this weird intuition when it comes to me," I tell him suspiciously. "I don't know how you do it, but it's like you can see into my head. Every activity you choose for us is amazing."

"I think I'm just getting lucky," he admits as he puts aside the empty tray of cheese. "It seems like I'm putting all this effort into choosing events specifically for you—but we might just genuinely like the same things."

"And maybe I'm just easy to please?" I say in a seductive tone, moving closer to him.

"Maybe," he says, reaching out to slide his hands around my hips, "but I think I still have a lot to find out about that." Lowering his lips to mine,

CLARITY 2

he kisses me deeply. His hands slide around my back as he angles his face for better access to my mouth.

His touch makes me feel dizzy. Combined with too many wine tastings, I almost feel like I might fall over. He senses my unsteadiness and pushes me back against the balcony railing. I gasp a little, afraid of the considerable plunge to dozens of stories below. I cannot see the drop, so I imagine the street to be an enormous distance away—maybe hundreds of miles below. His kiss makes me feel like I am falling even though I am standing still. We must be up in the stratosphere, for I am having difficulty breathing. The air is thin up here. All I can taste is Liam—I seem to be breathing in his skin. The scent of his cologne and the sweetness of his lips make me more light-headed than any wine or drug possibly could. I still feel like I am falling, directly through the atmosphere now. There is a heat blossoming inside me. My heart is pounding fiercely, and I really feel like I might somehow be in outer space. I can no longer feel the familiar tug of gravity weighing me down. I cling to Liam, somewhat terrified of the vast expanse of space below; but I trust that he won't let me hit the ground. His arms are wrapped tightly around my waist, and they grip me with certainty and protectiveness. I continue to kiss him, allowing my body to melt against his rock-hard frame, holding him desperately for stability. I fear that if I let go, I'll go hurtling out into some infinite abyss.

"Hey!" says someone stepping out on the balcony. "Liam, isn't she your patient? What are you doing, bro?"

"Well..." he says nervously, hesitating. His voice sounds faraway and confused. I know that whatever distant place to which my mind had been flung, he was there with me.

"It's my fault," I say, trying to gather my composure and pull myself away from Liam. "I've had way too much to drink, and I forced myself on him. Just consider him my helpless victim."

The intruder laughs. "You're wild, Winter. Come on back inside. We just opened up some more wines I think you'll love."

When he disappears, I sigh in relief. "I'm sorry, Liam."

He pulls me close again and places a few more kisses on my lips. "Worth the risk," he whispers.

"Come on," I tell him, grabbing his hand and leading him inside. "I'm going to tell your friends the story about how I lost my virginity among the grape vines, when I was only twelve years old. To a French kid named Pierre."

"Is that true?" Liam asks in shock.

"Maybe. Maybe not." I shrug mischievously. "Who cares? I'm a writer and it will make for a really great story."

CLARITY 2

Chapter Eleven

The car driving along the highway feels as smooth as though it might be a boat cruising through water. I have no idea what time it is, but it's very, very late. The party ran into the early hours of the morning, and Liam needed some time to sober up before driving. Owen and Caroline were so drunk that they were nearly unconscious, and it took some considerable effort to stuff them into the car. Luckily, by the time Liam drove to their apartment, they were conscious enough to walk and use the elevator on their own.

Now, I am sitting in Liam's passenger seat as he ferries me home. I am imagining that we are in a yacht, steering through the rocky waves of the ocean. Every bump in the road feels like a large swell of water rocking the boat. My head rolls from side to side slightly, and I acknowledge that I am also somewhat drunk—but the perfect amount of intoxication. The world seems a little more magical, but I haven't completely lost my senses.

"Is it normal how Owen and Caroline argue

about everything?" I ask Liam. "They only seem to get along when their lips are connected."

"Their attraction is mostly a physical one," Liam explains. "They do seem strange to the uninformed onlooker. But they have their own... language. Underneath all of that craziness, they really are good friends."

"I like them," I say to him with a lazy smile. I reach out and try to touch his leg, but my hand accidentally drifts a bit too far up his thigh. I giggle to myself a little. "And I really like you."

"Winter," Liam says with warning, clearing his throat. "I'm driving."

"Mmm, am I distracting you?" I ask sleepily. I let my hand brush against his manhood, stirring him to life. I suddenly feel curious and explorative, like when I was swirling the glass of wine within my hand. I trace my fingers in a teasing circular pattern along the front of his pants.

"Whoa," he says, his voice suddenly hoarse. "Remind me to give you wine more often. It makes you really bold."

"Yeah," I murmur, releasing my seatbelt. "I feel so good. Like nothing bad has ever happened. Like nothing bad ever could happen. I feel no pain. I feel like I can see all the colors in the whole world. I feel like I'm floating. Floating over the water with you."

"The water?" Liam asks in confusion.

"Yes," I say, leaning over to rest my face

CLARITY 2

against his shoulder. I snuggle closer to him and wrap my arms around his torso. I let my hands caress his firm abdominals which must have been developed from plenty of judo. "In the boat," I explain sleepily, "over the water."

"Okay," he says with a little laugh.

I doze off against his shoulder, until I find him gently shaking me. To my surprise, the car has stopped moving. It feels like I was barely asleep for a second, but several minutes must have passed.

"We're here," Liam tells me softly. "At your house."

"Dammit," I say, sobering up almost instantly. It's time to cautiously sneak up into my bedroom once again while trying to avoid Grayson. Even though I feel very weak and sleepy, I will also have to slide my dresser in front of my door. I release a loud yawn. "At least he's unlikely to be awake at this hour," I assure myself. "So the coast should be clear."

"You'll be fine," Liam says, caressing my hair. He places a kiss on my forehead. "Just ignore that asshole. He can't hurt you anymore."

I nod in agreement.

"I'll open your door for you," Liam says. He pulls away from me and exits through his side of the vehicle.

I feel cold due to the sudden removal of his body heat, and I pull my coat closer around me.

Loretta Lost

When my door opens and he offers me his hand, I accept it and step outside with a smile. "This was a really great night," I tell him, "as always. Thanks for inviting me out."

"We're going to have a lot of amazing nights," he assures me. "I love spending time with you. I want to take you everywhere. I want to experience everything with you."

"I'd like that," I say softly, reaching for his tie to tug him down for a goodnight kiss.

Liam responds with gusto. He holds nothing back as he dives into my lips, whisking me away to that outer space again, almost instantly. I am not sure how he does it. No one has ever had this effect on me. I am dazed with pleasure when he plasters my body against the side of his car and slowly presses kisses along my chin and neck. His touch sends shivers of excitement directly through me, converging at my center. In an effort to be closer to him, I hook one of my legs around his, pulling him tighter against my body as I wrap my arms around his neck and kiss him deeply.

"I wish you didn't have to go," Liam groans between kisses.

"Me too," I whisper.

"This feels right, doesn't it?" Liam asks me. "You and me?"

I sigh and murmur against his mouth. "Yes. Definitely."

"Soon," he says quietly, pressing his lips

CLARITY 2

against my cheek and then my earlobe. "Once we get past this doctor-patient stuff, I'll make you mine. And I'll keep you for good."

"I'm impatient," I say, tugging on his tie again. "I want to be yours now."

"But Winter..."

"Stop talking and kiss me," I command him.

He does not hesitate to comply. He slips his hand behind my head, letting his fingers get tangled up in my hair as he kisses me soundly. He lets his other hand trail over my collarbone and underneath the neckline of my blouse. I feel his fingers exploring downward to trace the edge of my bra. The sensitive, warm skin there responds to the cold and gentle touch of his fingers, and I arch my back to encourage him. He tenderly cups my breast in his hand and begins to massage my flesh. A small moan escapes my lips, and I am about to give him permission and beg him for more when I am startled by the noise of a door slamming. Liam rips his hands away from my body, and straightens himself.

For a moment, I am worried that it's my dad. I feel like a teenager terrified that my father has caught me fooling around in the car with my boyfriend. Then, I recall the greater threat. I am too stunned, being brutally yanked out of my bliss, to properly register the danger.

"Get the fuck away from her!" Grayson shouts as he moves toward us.

Loretta Lost

I feel like ice has been poured into my spine. I am suddenly frozen and unable to move.

"Relax, man!" Liam says. "Just relax. Helen is an adult, and she can do whatever she wants."

"I said to get the fuck away from her!" Grayson yells again, his voice rising to a fanatical screech.

My stomach contorts with nausea at the loathsome sound of his voice.

"Get in the car," Liam whispers to me, opening the door and swiftly guiding me inside. "Duck down below the glass."

When he shuts the car door, I follow his instructions and lean forward, lowering my head and torso. Only after I am crouching below the protection of the metal panel do I realize why he has asked me to do this. Grayson's gun. Just as I realize what's happening, the deafening sound of a shot being fired causes me to jump. I no longer care about my own safety, and I grab the handle of the car door and try to swing it open.

"Liam!" I scream in horror.

"Stay down!" he yells at me, shoving the car door closed again. "I'm fine!"

Another earsplitting shot is fired, and I flinch as I feel the glass window above me shatter. My heart sinks as I imagine Liam shot and bleeding to death a few feet away, outside the car.

"Who the fuck do you think you are?" Grayson shouts. "Keeping her out all night and

CLARITY 2

treating her like your little whore?"

Another shot is fired, but this time I hear Grayson grunting in pain. There seems to be some sort of struggle, and the sound of a metal item clattering to the floor. There is a loud thump followed by Grayson howling bloody murder.

Another gunshot.

Everything goes quiet.

"Liam?" I whisper fearfully. With a shaking hand I reach for the handle and push open the car door. I swing my legs out, causing pieces of the shattered glass window to fall from my lap and clatter to the ground. I move forward in a daze, afraid of what I'll discover. I take a few more tentative steps before my toes collide with a motionless body. I stand completely still, staring down in shock. I wish I could see the scene before me so I didn't have to crouch down on my hands and knees and try to identify the lifeless man on the ground.

This can't be happening. Liam was laughing with me and kissing me just a moment before. I have only just found him, and the thought of losing him like this rips my heart in half.

I can't lose him before I have ever had the chance to really call him mine.

Please, God. Don't let him be gone.

"Liam?" I say softly again, into the emptiness of the night. I can feel my frosty breath tickle my lips. I wait. Nothing. No response. Tears spring to my eyes. The panic in my chest builds to a feverish scream as my voice bursts out of my chest like one of the gunshots echoing into the distance. *"Liam!"*

Book #3 will be released soon!

Subscribe to Loretta's mailing list to be informed of new releases.

www.LorettaLost.com

Connect with the author:

Facebook: facebook.com/LorettaLost
Twitter: @LorettaLost
Website: www.LorettaLost.com
Email: Loretta.lost@hotmail.com